A Sweet Scent of Death

GUILLERMO ARRIAGA

Translated from the Spanish by
JOHN PAGE

WASHINGTON SQUARE PRESS
New York   London   Toronto   Sydney

Washington Square Press
A Division of Simon & Schuster, Inc.
1230 Avenue of the Americas
New York, NY 10020

This book is a work of fiction. Names, characters, places,
and incidents either are products of the author's imagination
or are used fictitiously. Any resemblance to actual events or
locales or persons, living or dead, is entirely coincidental.

Copyright © 1994 by Guillermo Arriaga
Translation copyright © 2002 by John Page

Originally published in Mexico in 1994
as Un dulce olor a muerte by Grupo Editorial Planeta
Translation originally published in Great Britain in 2002
by Faber and Faber Limited

All rights reserved, including the right to reproduce
this book or portions thereof in any form whatsoever.
For information address Atria Books Subsidiary Rights Department,
1230 Avenue of the Americas, New York, NY 10020

First Washington Square Press trade paperback edition April 2007

WASHINGTON SQUARE PRESS and colophon are registered
trademarks of Simon & Schuster, Inc.

For information about special discounts for bulk purchases,
please contact Simon & Schuster Special Sales at
1-800-456-6798 or business@simonandschuster.com

Manufactured in the United States of America

1   3   5   7   9   10   8   6   4   2

ISBN-13: 978-0-7432-9679-3
ISBN-10:   0-7432-9679-6

CHAPTER I

Adela

1

Ramón Castaños was dusting his counter when he heard a faraway, piercing shriek. Listening carefully, he heard only the usual morning hum. He decided it was just the screech of a chachalaca, many of which flapped about the hill. He went on with his dusting. Taking down a shelf, he prepared to clean it, when there was another scream, much closer and clearer. This was followed by another, then another. Ramón put down the shelf, jumped over the counter and went out the door to see what was happening. It was early Sunday; he found no one. But the screams became more and more frantic and continuous. Walking out to the middle of the street, he saw three boys in the distance, running towards him, shouting at the top of their lungs.

'A dead woman . . . a dead woman . . .'

Ramón moved toward them and stopped one as the others fled among the houses. 'What's up?' he asked.

'They killed her . . . they killed her . . .' howled the boy.

'Who? Where?'

Without another word the child raced off, back where he'd come from. Ramón followed him, running along the path to the river, until they reached a field of sorghum.

'There,' gasped the frightened child, pointing to one side of the field.

A corpse lay among the furrows. Ramón approached

slowly, his heart pounding at every step. The woman was nude, lying face up in a pool of blood. The moment he saw her he could not take his eyes off her. At sixteen he had often dreamt of seeing a naked woman, but had never imagined finding one like this. He surveyed her smooth, motionless skin more in shock than in lust, for it was a young body. With her arms stretched back and one leg slightly bent, she seemed to implore a final embrace. The sight moved him. He swallowed hard and took a deep breath, noticing the sweet scent of cheap floral perfume. He felt like giving her his hand, lifting her, telling her to cut out the pretense of death. She remained nude and still. Ramón took off his shirt, his Sunday best, and covered her as well as he could. As he bent over, he recognized Adela. She had been stabbed in the back.

2

A crowd of curious villagers, led by the other kids, arrived noisily, almost stumbling over the body. But the sight of it silenced them. They surrounded it quietly, some furtively examining the dead woman. Ramón realized that her body was still partly exposed. He broke off a few sorghum stalks to cover the bare parts. The others watched him, surprised, as if intruding on a private rite.

A fat, gray-haired man pushed his way to the front. He was Loma Grande's ejido delegate, Justino Téllez. He stopped momentarily, reluctant to go beyond the circle surrounding Ramón and the dead girl. He would have preferred to stay out of the way, in the crowd, but he represented authority and as such would have to intervene. Taking three steps forward, he spat on the ground and

4

said something to Ramón which no one heard. He knelt beside the body, raising the shirt to look at the girl's face.

He crouched, examining the corpse for some time. Finally, covering it again, he stood up with difficulty and clicked his tongue. With a bandanna from his pocket he wiped the sweat trickling down his face.

'Bring a cart,' he ordered. 'We have to take her to the village.'

No one moved. Aware that he was not being obeyed, Justino Téllez examined the faces watching him and stopped at Pascual Ortega, thin, awkward and bowlegged. 'Move it, Pascual; go get your grandfather's cart.'

As if he had been brusquely awakened, Pascual took one look at the corpse, then at the delegate, swung around and dashed off to Loma Grande.

Justino and Ramón stood wordlessly face to face. Among the whispers of the curious, someone asked, 'Who is she?'

No one really knew who she was, but an unidentified voice declared, 'Ramón Castaños' girl.'

A buzz of murmurs rose, then stopped, leaving a heavy silence, broken only by chirping cicadas. The sun began to bake the air, raising humid heat from the ground. There was not a breath to cool the inert flesh lying before them.

'She wasn't stabbed very long ago,' murmured Justino. 'She isn't stiff, and there aren't any ants yet.'

Ramón looked at him, bewildered. Téllez continued even more quietly, 'She was killed less than two hours ago.'

Pascual returned with the cart and parked it as close to the victim as possible. The circle drew back, but remained expectant for the long time it took Ramón to decide to put his arms under the corpse and lift it. Unexpectedly one of his hands touched the sticky wound and, repelled, he moved it brusquely. The shirt and stalks fell away, leaving the woman nude again. And again morbid eyes stared at the exposed skin. Ramón made an effort to spare Adela's vulnerable modesty by turning his back on the crowd and walking away across the furrows. The onlookers yielded with no effort to help him. Stumbling, he approached the cart and gently deposited the supine figure. Pascual handed him a blanket with which to cover her.

Justino came up to make sure that all was well and ordered, 'Take her away, Pascual.'

The boy took the driver's seat and whipped up the mules. The cart staggered along, shaking the body on its boards, followed by the crowd. The rumor was confirmed among those in the funeral procession: Ramón Castaños' girl had been murdered.

Justino and Ramón stood watching the cortège move away. Still affected by his brush with that warm flesh, Ramón felt his veins burning. He missed the weight of what he had just carried, feeling as if he had lost something that had always belonged to him. He looked at his arms, marked by faint bloodstains, and closed his eyes. He was suddenly seized by a dizzying need to chase after Adela and embrace her. The idea upset him and he felt faint.

Justino's voice brought him out of it. 'Ramón,' he said.

Ramón opened his eyes. The sky was a cloudless blue,

the rust-colored stands of sorghum ready for harvest, and death was the memory of a woman in his arms.

Justino bent down to pick up the shirt still lying on the ground. He handed it to Ramón, who automatically accepted it. It too was stained with blood. Rather than put it on, Ramón tied it around his waist.

The delegate scratched his head. 'I've got to admit,' he said, 'I'm damned if I know who that woman is.' Ramón sighed softly. He might have said the same. He had seen her no more than the five or six times she had come to buy at his store. Since then, he had found her very attractive. She was tall, with light eyes, so he had asked around for her name, and it was Juan Carrera who told him it was Adela. That was all he knew about her, but now that he had held her close to him, so naked and so close, he seemed to have known her all his life.

'Adela,' murmured Ramón. 'Her name was Adela.'

The delegate frowned; the name meant nothing to him.

'Adela,' repeated Ramón, as if the name pronounced itself.

'Adela what?' asked Justino.

Ramón shrugged his shoulders. The delegate looked down and examined the spot where the corpse had rested, now the site of a large bloodstain. Footprints were barely visible among the hardened, cracked lumps of earth. Justino followed them into the sorghum until they disappeared in the direction of the river. He squatted and measured the footprints by handspans. One of the prints measured one span: Adela's. Another measured a span and three fingers: the murderer's. Her prints were barefoot, his those of a high-heeled cowboy boot.

Justino took a breath and made his decision: 'Her killer was neither tall nor short, fat nor thin, right?'

7

Ramón assented, almost involuntarily. He hadn't listened.

Justino moved a little earth with his shoe and continued, 'He killed her with a long sharp knife, because he cut through her heart with one stab.' He scanned the place in search of a weapon. Not finding one, he continued: 'She fell face down, but the killer turned her over to see her face and left her that way . . . as if in the middle of a sentence.'

A flock of white-winged doves flew over them. Justino followed them with his eyes until they were lost on the horizon. 'She was a very young victim,' he said as if to himself. 'Why the hell would he want to kill her?'

Ramón didn't even turn to look at him. Justino Téllez spat on the ground, took him by the arm and began to walk him along the path.

CHAPTER II

The School

1

They returned to Loma Grande to find the cortège waiting for them, motionless around the cart, Adela's corpse swelling under the sun and dust. Other neighbors had joined the group. Among them, the word spread that Ramón Castaños' girl had been murdered.

Jacinto Cruz, butcher, and grave-digger in the village cemetery, approached Ramón. 'What's to be done?' he asked.

Irritated, Justino interposed; as local authority, it was he who should have been asked.

'Take her to the school,' he ordered.

Jacinto accepted the order, and when he was about to withdraw in compliance, the delegate stopped him.

'And tell the girl's parents.'

Jacinto Cruz looked at him inquisitively. 'And who are they?'

Téllez shrugged his shoulders and turned to Ramón, expecting a reply, but he didn't know either.

'I know them,' said Evelia, Lucio Estrada's wife. 'They live two lots beyond Macedonio Macedo's house.'

A few months before, Macedonio's house had marked the end of Loma Grande, but so many people kept coming from elsewhere to the village that its boundaries changed from week to week.

'Well, do me the favor, Evelia,' said Téllez in his hoarse voice; 'tell them what's happened.'

The body was taken to the school and, unintentionally, Ramón headed the funeral procession. The crowd did not move until he took the first step.

They laid her out on the floor of one of the only two classrooms, putting her on a straw mat so that she would get no dirtier, and left her covered with Pascual's blanket. Someone lit four votive candles, one at each corner of the mat, as the classroom began to get crowded. People pushed and shoved to position themselves as close as possible to the action. In spite of the tension, they never encroached on the space occupied by Ramón, as if it were marked by some invisible barrier.

2

In the midst of the crowd and the heat, Pedro Salgado, Ramón's cousin, came up to him.

'I'm so sorry about your girl, cousin,' he said.

Ramón looked at him in confusion. 'What girl?'

Pedro embraced him, exhaling a breath heavily laden with alcohol.

'I feel for you, cousin,' he whispered in Ramón's ear. Releasing him, he removed his shirt and gave it to Ramón.

'Here, so you don't walk around bare at a difficult time like this.'

Ramón realized that he was not wearing his own.

'No thank you,' he said, embarrassed, pointing to the shirt around his waist; 'I have my own.'

Pedro looked at him with unfocused eyes. He opened his mouth and slapped his chest.

'Cousin, your shirt's dirty, and I'm giving you mine with all my heart.'

Bewildered, Ramón took the shirt and thanked him for the favor. His cousin responded with a pat on his back.

'Whatever you need, Ramón,' he said with eyes on the verge of tears, kissing his cousin on the forehead. 'I know you loved her very much,' he murmured, stumbling away.

Ramón tried to catch up with him to make it clear that Adela had never been his girl and was a stranger to him as to everyone else, but the crowd prevented him. His only consolation was that his cousin was drunk.

'He didn't know what he was talking about,' thought Ramón.

He looked at Pedro's shirt. It smelled slightly of sweat and beer, but it was cleaner than his own, so he put it on and buttoned it up. It was a size larger than his.

Less than an hour after the murder was discovered the rumor of Ramón Castaños' girlfriend's death had spread to every corner of Loma Grande.

Crowded around the school, the villagers tried to find out about Ramón's relationship with the strange girl. Some took advantage of the opportunity to brag. Juan Carrera boasted that he had been a friend of the dead girl when in truth he had only wished her a 'Good day' one distant Thursday in June, which Adela had not deigned to answer.

'I introduced her to Ramón,' he maintained. 'Thanks to me they began to go steady.'

3

The widow Castaños was scaling tilapias she had received from Melquiades and Pedro Estrada, when she saw the funeral procession passing a few blocks away. She paid no attention, thinking it just another of the many religious processions organized by the evangelicals on Sunday mornings. She went back to her work, finished cleaning the mojarras and rinsed them to remove the last vestiges of gut. María Gaya and Eduviges Lovera arrived to tell her what had happened, just as she was finishing. They told the tale, interrupting each other constantly. The widow admitted she was surprised. She had never heard about a relationship between her son and this Adela, nor had Ramón ever confessed to having a girlfriend. The boy had never shown signs of the kind of craziness typical of people in love, the kind that might have given away a secret passion. No, that romance could not be true. She would never have missed something so important. However, her friends insisted Ramón was Adela's steady boyfriend and Adela had been murdered at dawn. The widow refused to believe the story. Eduviges Lovera suggested she accompany them to the school to see for herself. She accepted, dropped the fish into a bucket, sprinkled them with salt and covered them with a piece of cardboard to keep off the flies, and set off.

When she reached the classroom and discovered her son at one end of it, the widow lost all doubt about the truth of what her friends had told her. Ramón looked pained and sad, the way men look when they lose the woman they have truly loved.

The widow Castaños hesitated an instant, unsure whether to console the youngest of her children. She did not dare to do so. Ramón's face revealed a suffering that she would be unable to ease. Full of sorrow, she left the classroom.

4

People continued to arrive at the improvised wake. The room could hold no more, but those outside wanted to come in and those inside refused to leave. Everyone wanted to be there, to murmur about this relationship that had been cut short, to get a whiff of the corpse and butt in to someone else's sorrow.

To make more space inside the classroom, the onlookers removed desks, chairs, blackboard and anything else that got in their way. They were so careless that several desks were broken in half. Desperate, Margarita Palacios, the only teacher in Loma Grande and its environs, tried to restrain the turmoil. Gesturing frantically, she insisted, 'Get that girl out of here. It will scare my pupils and they won't want to come back to school.' But her protests were in vain; the adults paid no attention, more interested in the buzz of events than in the vehemence of her arguments. Meanwhile, the children, far from being frightened, seemed infected with the furor of their elders. Pressed against the classroom windows, they tried their utmost to explore this unusual situation.

In the midst of the turmoil, Justino Téllez finally faced the inevitable: Adela had been Ramón Castaños' girlfriend. At first he had refused to believe it, thinking it was only claptrap; but the phrase was repeated so often by so many mouths that he finally accepted it as true. He was then able to explain Ramón's confusion, his vacant stare, his tense jaw; but he could not understand why Ramón had not confessed the truth, nor why he had hidden his relationship with Adela.

As an ejido, rather than a police, official, Justino Téllez was not much concerned to find answers to his questions.

Instead, he faced Ramón, saying, 'You sure had it covered up.'

At first, Ramón did not realize that Justino was talking to him; but as the delegate stood staring straight at him, it finally dawned on him he had been addressed.

'Covered up what?' he asked, annoyed.

Justino smiled and pointed his jaw at the shape of Adela's corpse. 'That she was your girlfriend.'

The response froze Ramón. Stammering, he tried to deny it: 'No . . . she . . . I . . .'

But there was no time to say any more, because at that moment someone yelled, 'Here come the rangers!'

CHAPTER III

Carmelo Lozano

1

Two blue-gray pick-ups crunched to a halt in front of the school. Their arrival was violent and ostentatious, raising a cloud of dust and scaring the kids. Carmelo Lozano, chief of the rural police based at Ciudad Mante, got out of one of them. Carmelo was not in the habit of making rounds on Sundays, but that morning he had woken up with the conviction that something serious was happening around Loma Grande. 'I've got the vibes,' he said to his subordinates. He ordered them into the pick-ups and, following his instincts, led them without hesitation across forty kilometers of tangled dirt road to the village.

'Hi there, folks. What's all the fuss?' The villagers crowded around the classroom door fell back. Carmelo was not a bad man, nor was he good; he was a cop and that was reason enough to get out of his way.

Lozano had been able to see the corpse laid out in the classroom through one of the windows. He was delighted to corroborate his hunch; his 'vibes' had never failed him. He grabbed Guzmaro Collazos, an absent-minded youngster who had just arrived, by the shoulder.

'Who got killed, son?' asked Carmelo.

Guzmaro couldn't answer. He tried to break loose but Carmelo's huge hand held him tight.

'What's the matter? Tell me.'

Justino Téllez appeared in the doorway and changed the focus.

'First say hello, Captain . . . or have you forgotten your manners?'

Carmelo looked down at him from his six foot six and smiled. He and Justino had known each other since before Loma Grande was a village called Loma Grande, when it had been merely a four-house settlement. Carmelo let go of Guzmaro, who quickly got as far away from the policemen as he could, and walked towards Justino. They greeted each other as they had since they were boys.

'What's with you, beast with claws?' exclaimed Lozano.

Justino immediately answered, 'Just hanging out, beast with hoofs.'

Carmelo reached Justino and feinted a hook to the liver. The delegate pretended to dodge it.

'What's bitten you, Captain, to bring you all the way out here?'

'Nothing much, friend; just that I woke up with a yen to see your ugly face.'

Justino offered his hand and Carmelo gripped it in his.

'Well, now you have,' said Justino, 'you can go back where you came from.'

Carmelo raised his eyebrows. 'Ahhh . . . Justino, you're some number.'

The two stared at each other for a few seconds, then Téllez stepped forward.

'Come with me,' he said to the officer. 'There are too many ears around here waiting to hear what's none of their business.'

The curious around them drew back as if to escape the allusion. Lozano gestured his eight men to wait for him.

16

The two walked a few steps away into the shadow of a tall huisache.

'It seems, Carmelo,' said Téllez, as soon as he felt out of earshot, 'that a young thing has gone and died on us.'

'She died, or they died her?'

Justino spat on the loose earth and watched his spittle disappear into the dust.

'She was died ... malagueña-style: a knife in the back.'

With no change of expression, Carmelo smoothed his mustache and broke a twig off the huisache, to chew on.

'And who did they kill?'

Justino shook his head: 'I don't know. That's what I'm trying to find out.'

Carmelo shook his left arm to get rid of a grasshopper caught in his watch strap. The insect flew off towards the crowd watching them.

'Do you know who killed her?'

'Don't know that either.'

'About how old was the girl?' inquired Lozano.

Justino thought for a moment.

'I'm not much good at figuring ages, but I'd guess fifteen.'

Carmelo moistened his parched lips and wiped off the sweat beading his eyebrows.

'It sure is hot,' he said, staring at the heat waves shimmering along the street. 'So what do you think?' he continued. 'Doesn't it smell like a crime of passion?'

Téllez assented without conviction.

'These damned people, friend,' added Lozano. 'Nothing civilizes them. They still kill for no good reason at all.'

Justino looked at him in disbelief. In his youth, Lozano had badly wounded a woman out of sheer jealousy. She had survived the two slugs he put into her, and he, repentant, had proposed marriage. The woman accepted, but they never married. She had died of alcoholic congestion a few days before the wedding. Since then, he had considered any outburst of passion an act of barbarism.

'That's not "no good reason,"' argued Justino jokingly. 'Your problem is that you're old and don't understand these things any more.'

'It's your tail that's old,' rejoined Carmelo. He looked up at the sun, which seemed to vibrate in the sky. 'Shit,' he growled. 'I came all the way out here for nothing.'

Justino laughed sardonically. 'What did you expect, Captain? Contraband? A plane-load of grass?'

'Something worthwhile,' answered Lozano. 'Not a no-account killing.'

Justino knew that, deep down, what irritated Carmelo was the absence of anyone vulnerable to extortion, and without suspects or perpetrators there was no way to squeeze some money out of the affair. The crime and its victim concerned him not at all.

He licked his parched lips again. 'At least offer me a beer.'

Justino was on the verge of a ready 'Sure' when he remembered that, of the two stores in the village, the only one open on Sundays that sold cold beer belonged to Ramón.

'Can't be done.'

'No shit,' exclaimed Carmelo.

'There's no place to go,' explained Justino.

'How come?' asked Carmelo, rubbing the back of his neck.

'Because the victim was Ramón Castaños' girlfriend, and he owns the store around the corner.'

'Ramón? Francisca's son?'

'That's the one.' Carmelo smacked his tongue.

'Hey, didn't you say you didn't know who was killed?'

'Honestly, no. I never saw the girl before, and I don't know who she is. I've already told you the little I know, and I only found that out minutes ago.'

Lozano scratched his head, intrigued. 'Where's Ramón?'

'In there, at the wake,' answered Justino.

Carmelo threw away the huisache twig he'd been chewing.

'I can't even get a goddam beer. This isn't worth shit,' he complained. He took a ballpoint and a notebook out of his shirt pocket.

'What are you doing?' asked Justino.

'Gotta write a report.'

Justino snorted in disagreement. 'Don't shit me, Carmelo; leave things be. I'll handle it here and let you know what I find out.'

Lozano gave Justino a long look and slowly shook his head: 'Partner, why the hell do you stick your nose where it doesn't belong?'

'Hey, wait a minute,' exploded Justino. 'The last time you made one of your goddam reports we had the state troopers all over the village, only because you thought—'

Suddenly Carmelo interrupted him: 'Ramón killed her, right?'

Justino frowned, caught off balance.

'I knew it,' continued Lozano. 'That's jealousy for you, partner; no way to control it.'

CHAPTER IV

Adela Comes Back to Life

1

A shriek echoed across the four walls of the classroom: 'She's alive,' howled Prudencia Negrete. The old woman had seen the corpse twisting under the blanket.

Rosa León joined her with an even more strident howl: 'She's alive . . . she's moving . . .'

Ramón turned to look and felt a clawing sensation in his stomach; Adela was indeed moving: one of her sides was rising and falling slowly.

'Holy God, forgive us,' sobbed Gertrudis Sánchez, the only prostitute in Loma Grande and its environs, kneeling on the floor.

Lucio Estrada cut short the collective hysteria. 'Bunch of clowns,' he whispered in Ramón's ear. He walked to the body and uncovered it to the shoulders. Adela's peaceful expression of the morning had changed. Now her face seemed hardened, tense, about to scream.

'What do you mean, alive?' said Lucio sarcastically. 'All that heaving is because of the gases.'

Confused, Rosa León drew closer to verify what Lucio said, and when she was almost on top of the corpse, Lucio poked her in the ribs.

'Look out; she bites.'

Rosa León jumped back unsteadily as a number of people laughed out loud. But not Ramón. The sight of Adela, far more dead than before, affected him deeply. In a matter of seconds, Adela had changed before his eyes. No longer was she the warm woman he had carried in his arms, who had left him all confused. Now she was an enormous piece of meat. Even so, Adela seemed to stick to him, to swallow him, to subjugate him.

Lucio covered the body and spread out his arms, satisfied with his demonstration and with having ridiculed the hysterical women. Full of himself, he turned to chat with his friends while Rosa León sobbed as she left the classroom amid considerable laughter.

Prudencia's and Rosa's screams had caught everyone's attention, making them forget that nine rural policemen were waiting outside. They suddenly became aware of Carmelo Lozano and his men climbing into their pick-ups and Justino waving them off with a disgruntled flip of the hand.

The law departed as it had arrived: in a cloud of dust and scaring the kids.

Justino had managed to dispel Carmelo Lozano's suspicions of Ramón one by one. 'No, Captain, the boy isn't capable of something like this. We have both known him since he was little. How can you believe he would do something this awful?'

Justino's defense of the shopkeeper cost him a lot of jaw and a hundred pesos. 'For gas,' insisted Carmelo, 'and to buy me some ice-cold beer in Mante, since I was not properly received here.' Before he left, Lozano promised to return the following week 'to check out this unsolved matter' and, since he was not a bad man, he proved his good faith by the following report:

Sunday, 8 September 1991
Patrol carried out. Nothing of importance detected, nor crimes to pursue. The area in complete calm and good order.

Justino returned to the classroom and approached Ramón.

'I saved you from the lock-up,' he scolded, 'but you're going to have to explain all this mystery.'

2

The rays of the midday sun began to lick the village. The atmosphere in the classroom turned hot and clammy with the sweat and discharges of so many bodies. The concentrated odor of perspiration spared those present the bittersweet smell revealing the corpse's rapid decomposition. They became aware of it only when a dozen or so large green flies began to settle on the viscous ooze slipping beyond the edges of the straw mat.

'The flies are after her already,' pointed out Jacinto Cruz.

Justino Téllez approached the butcher. 'What do we do?' he asked.

Jacinto Cruz wrinkled his nose, the better to sniff and determine the body's degree of putrefaction.

'She has to be prepared quickly and put in a box,' he said calmly. 'She's well on her way.'

'Prepared', in Loma Grande, meant dressed, combed, made up, put in a coffin, given a brief farewell, a blessing, and into the grave. In summertime the dead ripened too quickly. However, such haste was not feasible: Evelia had not yet returned with Adela's parents. They would have to wait, and meanwhile find a way to protect the corpse from its own decay.

After turning the problem over a number of times, someone suggested the possibility of placing the body in ice. Only two people in the village used it: Lucio Estrada, to refrigerate fish, and Ramón, to chill Coca-Colas and beers. The idea didn't convince Lucio: the heat would melt the ice quickly and, mixed with blood, it would only cause a greater stench and attract more flies. Ramón didn't like it either. It made him dizzy just to imagine Adela chilled like a bottle of pop.

They forgot the ice. Tomás Lima, who at one time had worked in a pharmacy in Tampico, suggested injecting the body with formaldehyde. 'That will keep her,' he said. But the only formaldehyde available in Loma Grande belonged to Margarita Palacios, the teacher, and was used to preserve rabbit embryos in a mayonnaise jar.

It was unlikely the teacher would give up her ration. Besides the fact that she was offended by the uproar in her school, the floating fetuses constituted the keystone of her natural science class on Darwin's theory of evolution.

'Look,' she would say to her pupils as she shook the jar, 'they're just like fish.' Then she would puff out her cheeks and exclaim, 'But careful, they're baby rabbits,' and smile, satisfied with what she felt was a precise demonstration of the great scientist's thesis.

Indeed, the good teacher wasn't about to donate her ration of formaldehyde to the deceased, who was upsetting her school room, and even if she had been, it wouldn't have been enough – hardly four injections, whereas it would take three liters to embalm a body. Tomás Lima suggested 96° proof alcohol.

'Who has alcohol?' asked Justino Téllez aloud.

Two women responded and willingly went home to get it. Martina Borja returned quickly with half a liter in a white plastic container. Conradia Jiménez came back empty-handed under the impression the little she had put away had been consumed by her husband during one of his explosive binges.

Half a liter was not enough. Justino Téllez tried again: 'Does anyone else have any alcohol?'

Sotelo Villa remembered that he had seen a bottle of hydrogen peroxide among his belongings.

'Would that be any use?' he asked.

Tomás Lima thought for a moment and said, 'Well, it's better than nothing.'

So, Sotelo Villa brought the bottle of peroxide, Guzmaro Collazos some gentian violet, and Prudencio Negrete a little bottle of Merthiolate.

Tomás Lima grimaced.

'What's the matter?' asked Justino.

'That's still not enough to do the job,' he said.

Several other people went home in the hope of finding some kind of injectable medicine or preparation, but returned empty-handed.

Torcuato Garduño, who had been silent throughout the morning leaning in a corner, spoke up: 'Suppose we inject her with booze?'

Justino shot him an angry glance and was about to reprove him when Tomás Lima declared thoughtfully, 'It's alcohol, it might work.'

'Go for it,' said Torcuato with a grin, producing a pint from under his shirt which he passed to Tomás, who took it reverently, opened it, sniffed it and took a long pull.

'Shit,' he said with emotion, 'this is really good rum. You bet it'll work.'

They mixed the 96° proof alcohol with the peroxide, rum from a variety of bottles and the Merthiolate in an enamel pot.

After preparing the embalming fluid, the matter of how to inject it into the body arose. Amador Cendejas contributed a disposable syringe with a rusty needle he had found half-buried in his own corral, which he had used to vaccinate his goats several months before. Ethiel Cervera brought a yellowing biology text containing illustrations of the human anatomy so that they could find veins and arteries. Finally, who was to inject Adela?

'Will you do it?' Justino asked Tomás discreetly.

'No way, it gives me the willies . . . Let Ramón do it; she was his girl.'

One glance at Ramón and Justino realized the boy would never even take the syringe in his hands.

Justino offered the task to several others, who immediately declined: 'No, not me, my hand shakes.' 'What happens if I inject myself?' 'Won't Ramón get mad?'

In view of the shower of excuses, there was nothing for it but to enlist Torcuato Garduño, who was considered by all the villagers to be clumsy and careless.

In spite of his reputation, Torcuato revealed unusual skill in the handling of cadavers. He punctured the body with great skill and accuracy through the blanket and without exposing a single centimeter of naked skin. Following the illustrations in the biology book step by step, he introduced the needle by approximation, accurately finding the best channels through which to administer the fluid.

It took him several minutes under the eyes of numerous

attentive onlookers. When he had finished, he stood up perspiring, handed Tomás the syringe and rubbed his eyes.

'It feels like shit,' he said, his face livid and his mouth dry.

A sweet scent of alcohol, rum, death and perspiration hung in the air.

CHAPTER V

The Newcomers

1

Evelia finally showed up at four in the afternoon. She came along the hot, dusty street accompanied by Adela's parents: a woman in her fifties, all skin and bone, with a face wrinkled by the sun, and a tall old man, bald with pale eyes.

They reached the school and entered the classroom. The woman hurried to the body, uncovered it slowly but with obvious anxiety, and screamed at the sight of the face. The old man, seeing his wife's reaction, approached the corpse, closed his eyes and began to cry quietly.

Few in the village knew Adela's parents or even Adela. They were among the 'newcomers', the twenty or thirty campesinos who had arrived at Loma Grande from time to time, brought by the government from such far-off places as Jalisco, Guanajuato, Michoacán, to work land expropriated from drug-dealers that had been declared ejido. The old residents of Loma Grande avoided the 'newcomers', regarding them as intruders, outsiders, and opportunists who usurped plots that might well have belonged to them. The recent arrivals, mostly of humble origin and brought up in the most conservative traditions, were suspicious of the old residents, whose customs seemed strange and libertine to them. Thus, the two groups lived separate lives.

New or not, Adela's parents moved all those present.

Her mother, lying on the floor next to her daughter's body, moaned stifled lamentations. Crushed, her father seemed to shrink as he sat hugging his knees.

A weight of silence and heat hung over the classroom, a wordless vapor. No one looked straight ahead, only out of the corner of their eyes.

Justino discreetly beckoned Evelia.

'What took you so long?' he demanded softly.

Evelia panted as if she had made a great effort. 'They weren't home,' she answered. 'I found them cutting prickly pears on El Bernal.'

El Bernal was the only hill in the area, and to reach it from Loma Grande, one had to walk five kilometers through furrows, ravines, and underbrush.

'They didn't believe me,' continued Evelia. 'It took a lot of convincing to get them to come . . . they assured me that Adela had been in bed when they set out for the hill.'

'Asleep?' asked Justino thoughtfully.

'Yes,' assented Evelia.

'About what time did they leave the house?'

'A little before dawn, they said.'

The people around them listened attentively. Evelia was reputed to be a judicious woman, not given to fabrication. Whatever she said was considered true and credible. Evelia knew this and wasted few words; nor was she wasting words when she said, shortly, 'Someone killed the only daughter they had left.'

The sentence spread among the onlookers in a whisper. Hearing the news, some of them, a minority, were abashed at intruding on another's tragedy, and left the school. Others, the majority, became even more interested in witnessing the proceedings to the bitter end.

Sudden expressions of sympathy, ambiguous glances, cautious condolences, impertinent questions aroused in Ramón the conviction that what was said about his relationship with Adela was no longer a joke, or a rumor, but a new and definitive truth, which grew by the minute and required more and more effort to deny. Adela was becoming a trap and a mystery. His memory of her became confused. One by one, the images overlaid each other: Adela wearing a white blouse and yellow skirt, buying parsley in his store; Adela disappearing down the village streets; Adela naked, lying quietly in the silence of a sorghum field. Adela the murdered daughter, Adela soaked in blood, Adela soaking him with her blood. Adela reflected in her father's face, in her mother's pain. Adela, Adela, Adela. The Adela he had smelled and carried. Adela, the fear of Adela, the love for Adela. Who was Adela?

Concentrating as he was, Ramón was unaware that Adela's mother had stood up and was coming toward him. He did not discover her until they were face to face. It was then that he looked at her damp, wrinkled features scrutinizing his and he felt fear. She, seeming to guess it, softened her expression and said gently: 'Adela loved you very much . . .'

The remark hit Ramón like a solid punch. He wanted to get out of there, to leave Adela with her stench of death and the lie of their love, curse her mother, push her and yell at her to leave him in peace, flee the whirlpool of murmurs swallowing him up, put an end to the farce, announce that there was no truth in anything that was said about him and Adela.

Instead, in a languid voice which did not sound to him

like his own, Ramón said: 'So did I. I loved her very much too.'

3

Natalio Figueroa and his wife, Clotilde Aranda, had come to Loma Grande six months before, from a village called San Jerónimo, close to the city of León, Guanjuato. Adela was the youngest of their five children, all of whom were now dead. The oldest had died in their arms, of dysentery, at the age of four. The second had broken his neck at eleven, falling from a runaway horse. The third, a girl, had drowned at fourteen trying to cross the Rio Grande in the company of a boy with whom she had run off only a few days before. A stray bullet from a drunken brawl had smashed the head of their fourth as he walked past a cantina when he was nine.

'We don't know who stabbed Adela,' explained Justino, 'but we will find out soon enough.'

Natalio listened without looking at him. He breathed with difficulty, still unwilling to believe what had happened.

Natalio knew that sooner or later the name of his daughter's killer would be heard around the village. For the time being he was more concerned with other obligations than with finding out the circumstances of the crime. 'Is there no way we could get a priest?' he asked doubtfully. 'I want one to bless my Adela.'

Justino looked at him with a touch of pity: 'No, there is no way at all.'

The nearest priest was in Ciudad Mante and there was no transport to get there, the only two pick-up trucks in

Loma Grande having broken down, and the bus passing through only on Tuesday and Thursday afternoons. On horseback, the trip was too long and tiring, no less than ten hours each way. It would be impossible to bring a priest.

Justino said nothing about this to Natalio. Instead he said, 'We'll get one right away,' and sent someone to get the two evangelists living on the Pastores Ejido.

They, too, were a kind of priest, he thought: they also prayed and blessed.

Rodolfo Horner and Luis Fernando Brehm, both evangelists, were descendants of German merchants who had come to Mexico at the beginning of the century. They looked like father and son, but were not. Every Sunday they came to Loma Grande to preach, early in the morning, beating snare drum and tambourine, and shouting religious slogans that invited sinners to repent their evil ways. The first time they had arrived, there were few in the village who had attended more than one mass in their lifetime or could haltingly recite the Lord's Prayer. They had listened to the two with respect and deference. Touched, several gave them pigs, chickens, turkeys. Others, in the hope of gaining eternal forgiveness and avoiding the road to purgatory, confessed their sins. The evangelists heard them politely, explaining that they did not hear confession and did so now only to comfort the faithful, not because they thought it was necessary.

With the passage of time, the evangelists had begun to scold the sinners, threatening them with implacable chastisement by the divine fist. The villagers became bored and decided to make fun of them: Tomás Lima confessed he had killed eight men for sheer pleasure. Torcuato Garduño talked to them about the several flavors of human flesh

31

and Gertrudis Sánchez excited them with detailed descriptions of the love triangles she carried on with her brother and father.

It had taken them a while to discover the plot, but when they did, they were furious. They redoubled their threats and the villagers made even more fun of them. This did not deter them from preaching in Loma Grande every Sunday; and if they did not appear in the village on the Sunday Adela was murdered, it was because Rodolfo Horner, the younger of the two, had been stung by a scorpion.

When Pascual Ortega arrived to take them to the wake, they were delighted. It was the first time they had been asked to take part in a religious ceremony. After breaking their backs day after day, withstanding rejection, ridicule and long walks under the burning sun, their efforts were bearing fruit. However, when they found out they were to officiate for the soul of a woman murdered in shady circumstances, they backed out. They had no desire to get mixed up in other people's problems and tried to excuse themselves on the grounds that Rodolfo was still weak from the effects of the scorpion sting and might get worse if he rode a horse.

'The poison could go to his head,' explained Luis Fernando.

Pascual smiled sardonically: pure baloney. He had been stung by more than ten scorpions and knew that, outside of the choking sensation of having swallowed air, which lasted a few hours, and inflammation at the site of the sting, which disappeared in a week, nothing serious ever happened.

Pascual's sarcastic and challenging attitude suggested to the evangelists that their excuse was not entirely convincing. The choice was either spending the night inventing absurd pretexts, or going to Loma Grande and officiating as discreetly as possible, so as not to become involved in the crime.

They left the Pastores Ejido in the late afternoon, Pascual Ortega leading them to Loma Grande via the shortest route, which crossed the field of sorghum where Adela had been killed. As they passed the spot, Pascual pointed with his chin at a dark patch that was undefinable at that hour of the afternoon. 'That's where they killed her,' he declared.

The evangelists huddled in their saddles and murmured a few prayers for the salvation of her soul.

They reached the village at nightfall and found no one in the streets or the school. Adela's body had been taken to her parents' home.

CHAPTER VI

A Black Skirt and a Blue Blouse

1

As he entered Natalio Figueroa and Clotilde Aranda's house, Ramón looked it over. It was a poor dwelling: four walls at right angles, covered with a thatched roof. A single, undivided enclosure, with an adobe-block stove in the center, a cot on one side and a bed on the other; a table and three chairs, blue enamel plates, red plastic cups; greasy frying pans, the smell of burnt food; a large unpainted cupboard; illustrations of the Virgin of Guadalupe and the child Jesus; oil-lamp wicks in Nescafé jars; two windows: one north, the other south; two stained rags for curtains, and a threadbare sheet shrouding Adela stretched on the cot on which she had awoken for the last time.

Natalio pulled up a chair and offered it to Ramón, who thanked him and, making as if to sit, finally remained standing. Justino and Evelia sat on the other two chairs while Clotilde Aranda curled up among the blankets on the bed. Only these five remained inside the house. The other villagers gathered on the level ground around the house.

'Coffee?' asked Natalio of no one in particular. Justino and Ramón turned down the offer. Evelia, tired from so much running, not having eaten anything since morning, accepted it. Clotilde Aranda stood up to make the coffee. She wiped away her tears and stepped up to the stove, placed a clay pot over the still-glowing embers and blew on them to rouse a flame. She waited, her eyes fixed on the water, which slowly began to boil, while the others watched her in silence.

Steam began to rise from the coffee but Clotilde remained in the same position. Natalio gently shook her out of her absorption, startling her.

'What's the matter?'

Natalio stretched one of his bony hands toward the stove. 'The coffee . . . it's ready.'

Clotilde looked at the pot, hung her head and began to moan: 'Adela . . . my Adela . . .'

Natalio rose and put his arm around her, leading her to the bed and helping her lie down.

Ramón had difficulty breathing. Exuding death, Adela seemed to steal the air in that cramped room, rarefying it.

'Don't you want any coffee?'

Ramón raised his eyes to the voice and looked at the cup Natalio was waving in front of him. No, he didn't want any coffee. What he wanted was to flee, to run as far as he could, until he burst. To flee as fast as possible from that huge body that was Adela.

'Thank you,' he said, receiving the steaming cup with both hands.

He took a sip and sat in the chair Natalio had offered him earlier.

2

After whimpering for a long time, Clotilde recovered her composure and set about looking for clothes in which to dress Adela for her burial. She opened the cupboard and examined its contents carefully. She took out two blouses and looked again, as if for something she had lost. Desperately, she emptied the cupboard and inspected its contents one by one. Finally she bit her lip and twisted her face towards her husband.

'Her black skirt and blue blouse aren't here,' she said, defeated.

They were Adela's best, her favorite outfit. She had used them only on two occasions she had considered very special: the first, when she had turned fifteen and her birthday had been celebrated with the traditional presentation dance in San Jerónimo; and the second, the day she had received her grade school diploma. She had not worn them again until that Sunday.

Clotilde's depression worsened at not finding the black skirt and blue blouse. She had planned to dress her daughter in them for the funeral. Disconsolate, she leaned against the empty cupboard, nodding her head back and forth.

Natalio approached his wife, picking up the articles of clothing on the floor and setting aside a white blouse and a yellow skirt.

'Put these on her,' he said, handing them to her.

Clotilde accepted them as if they were of great value; she held them to her breast and caressed them longingly.

In the semi-darkness, Ramón became aware of what the woman held in her hands, and an icy shiver welled up from deep inside him: they were the same clothes Adela had worn the afternoon he had first seen her. And again, Adela took hold of him, the other Adela, the one with clear eyes, a fresh glance, a smooth neck, a slightly hoarse voice and an imperceptible laugh. Adela again, fragile, naked, silent, he holding her and she scorching him. And Adela and the enormous body that was Adela. And Ramón and the two Adelas, and Adela dead. Far too dead.

3

Clotilde Aranda was helpless. She could not face the swollen flesh and bone she had once called her daughter. She dared not looked at her. Much less touch her. She was unable to dress her, unable to comb her tangled hair, unable to caress her, to remove the smile of death from her lips. Natalio looked at his defeated wife. She had fulfilled to the last the arduous task of preparing and shrouding all her other dead children. But shrouding Adela implied shrouding a piece of herself, all that she had left of hope.

Silently, Natalio took the white blouse and yellow skirt from his wife's hand and held them out to Evelia. Though she immediately understood the meaning of the gesture, she was too tired to face what was being asked of her, and could not find it in herself to refuse. She took the garments, half-closed her eyes and asked: 'What shoes shall I put on her?'

Natalio turned to his wife in search of an answer.

Clotilde shook her head. Adela owned only one pair of shoes and had, undoubtedly, worn them that morning.

'She hasn't any,' answered the mother, ashamed.

Evelia remained alone with the body. She sat on the edge of the cot, took a last sip of coffee, ruffled her hair and sighed. Taking a corner of the sheet that covered Adela, she removed it slowly. Free of its temporary shroud, the naked body gave off a penetrating odor that stung Evelia's nostrils. She quickly covered them with her hand. The rush of pestilence quickly dissipated in the darkness, leaving a faint smell of vinegar in the room. The corpse's skin, dried by the concoction injected into it, felt like cardboard. Violet stripes marked arms and legs; but the face had acquired a serene expression as if Adela was finally resting from all the confusion she herself had caused.

Evelia raised her eyes to avoid being overcome by the sight of the corpse. She tried to think of something entirely different, but to no avail: there was too much death in the room. She realized that by herself she would not be able to prepare Adela. She pushed herself away from the cot with her hands. Standing, she shrugged her shoulders and stepped out the door.

Natalio approached her hurriedly. 'Is she ready?' he asked nervously.

'No, not yet . . . I need someone to help me.'

Evelia took a step forward, searching among the dozens of shadows around her. She looked them over slowly. Close to the wire fence bordering the property she made out the silhouettes of Astrid Monge and Anita Novoa, two girls who lived nearby, whom she had known since they were children. She had seen them both occasionally with Adela.

Evelia called them and they came, impelled by curiosity.

'Will you help me dress her?' she asked the two faces dimmed by the night.

For a few seconds she heard only the girls' breathing as they made up their minds.

'Not me,' answered Anita shortly.

Evelia turned to Astrid and in the darkness divined a slight nod of the head.

They went back into the house in silence. By the faint light of the oil wicks, Astrid could see the corpse lying on the cot. A cloud of flies buzzed over Adela's half-opened eyes, trying to drink her last tears. A thick nausea rose in Astrid's throat and reached her palate. She wanted to spit out not only her revulsion but her fury as well: fury at the flies, at so much silence, at Adela's obstinate stillness.

Evelia shook a rag to chase off the flies, which dispersed briefly and then returned to settle on the dead girl's eyes.

'Help me raise her,' she said to Astrid.

Astrid clenched her teeth and fists to give her strength. Plucking up courage, and with extreme care, she put her hands on Adela's back. Barely grazing the rough skin, she became aware of the great difference between touching death and just looking at it. She discovered that what was lying there was not Adela – at least not the Adela she had known for the last few months and with whom she had become close friends. Not the Adela with whom she had talked, laughed and confessed secrets. Not the Adela of the transparent glance. No, that pasty, cardboard mass was not Adela.

'Don't get upset,' said Evelia warmly, seeing her confusion, 'because if you do, so will I, and there won't be anyone to dress her.'

'I'm all right,' answered Astrid sadly. 'It's just that I can't get used to seeing her like this.'

Evelia showed her the blouse. 'We've got to hurry.'

Astrid smoothed Adela's hair. 'The other day she asked me to braid her hair,' she said with the same sadness.

In the distance, they could hear the blows of a hammer.

'She was in love,' she said, still caressing the hair.

'In love with whom?' asked Evelia.

'I don't know.'

'With Ramón?'

'Who knows? I don't.'

Astrid could not go on. Pressing her lips together, she

held back her tears and resolutely raised the cardboard body so that they could begin to dress it.

Jacinto Cruz finished hammering, and sanded the wood on the inside of the coffin. He had built it with boards left over from the abandoned house in which Jeremías Martínez had lived out the last years of his life. That house supplied most of the coffins required in Loma Grande.

Pascual rode up on his cart, ready to pick up the coffin. He jumped down and approached Jacinto.

'I've brought the priests,' he said, meaning the evangelists, 'and she's all dressed and ready to go. All that's missing is the coffin.'

'And the grave,' added Jacinto.

Pascual smiled without really wanting to. He walked around the coffin, inspecting it carefully.

'Hey, didn't you make it sort of big?'

Jacinto looked over his work and shook his head.

'No, it's the right size.'

Pascual took two paces.

'It's two paces long,' he said, 'and the girl wasn't that long.'

Jacinto looked up at the moonless sky and slowly turned toward Pascual. 'They say the dead, the more they die, the bigger and wider they get.'

'Yeah, so they say,' murmured Pascual.

He grabbed the coffin at one end and motioned to Jacinto to pick up the other.

CHAPTER VII

The Murderer

1

They buried Adela in the old cemetery on the banks of the Guayalejo river, near the place where she had been murdered. They dug a deep grave so that she would not be uncovered and dragged away when the river rose in the rainy season. For many of the villagers it was the saddest funeral they had ever attended, more so even than that of Doña Paulita Estrada or Don Refugio López, founders of the village. There were no cries or lamentations, just silence and a moonless night.

Caught up in the general depression, the evangelists limited themselves to a brief farewell and a short blessing. The ceremony over, the villagers dispersed in tight groups, heading toward Loma Grande in the darkness that covered the trails overgrown with weeds.

Most of the men followed Ramón to the store. There was still a lot to be cleared up and no better way to do it than with cold beer in hand.

Ramón knew perfectly well that for him the night was barely beginning. Caught as he was in an invisible love affair, there was no way he could back out and deny the romance without being accused of cowardice and of being less than a man. From then on he would have to live that imaginary past as reality.

2

Nothing was ever resolved directly or unequivocally in Loma Grande, not even crime. First a web of pointless conversation would, little by little, have to be woven towards the heart of the matter. It was for this reason that Justino Tellez, after bolting a gulp of beer to refresh his gullet, asked Lucio Estrada how much the government was paying per ton of sorghum.

'Three hundred and fifty pesos,' answered Lucio, somewhat irritated.

'That doesn't even pay for the seed,' broke in Torcuato Garduño.

'Let alone the rental of the threshing machines,' added Amador Cendejas.

'That's why I don't grow it any more,' said Ranulfo Quirarte, nicknamed 'Old Friendly' for his habit of striking up conversation with anyone, anywhere, and who made his living selling the meat of deer he shot at night by dazzling them from a bicycle and shooting them remorselessly with a 16-gauge double-barreled shotgun.

'We aren't going to plant any either,' declared Melquiades, Lucio and Pedro Estrada's younger brother. 'We're going into the fish biz.'

'We've bought four nets to set in the reservoir reeds,' added Lucio.

'Is there a lot of mojarra there?' inquired Justino Tellez.

'Lots,' confirmed Melquiades. 'We caught two hundred kilos last week.'

'Are you still filleting them?' asked Justino.

'Not any more,' answered Lucio. 'Not since my filleting knife was stolen.'

'Which one?'

'The knife Mr Larre gave me; it was long, thin and sharp.'

'Larre?'

'Yeah, the hunter who comes from Mexico City to shoot goose. A tall heavy-set guy.'

'Ahh, yes.' Justino took another mouthful of beer, rinsed several times and spat it out.

'What about the knife? Who do you think stole it from you?'

Lucio grinned at the question. 'I don't know. If I did, I would have taken it away from him.'

'Well I wish you knew,' continued Justino Téllez, ''cause I've got a hunch that was the knife that killed the girl.'

Lucio and the rest fell silent. Ramón remembered seeing it. Justino was right: only a knife of that size and edge could have cut through Adela so cleanly.

Torcuato Garduño changed the subject.

'Well, I've got a feeling,' he said, looking southward, 'it's going to start raining next week.'

'For sure,' continued Macedonio; 'there seems to have been a breeze from the Huasteca for the last three days.'

'A little water wouldn't hurt,' said Amador Cendejas; 'it would help the sorghum grow.'

'Goddam sorghum,' interrupted Torcuato. 'If I'd known they were paying three-fifty, I'd never have planted.'

'We should have planted safflower seed, like Ethiel,' said Pedro Salgado.

'Yeah, right,' declared Justino. 'A ton of safflower is worth twice that; but we planted sorghum, so we're stuck with it.'

Conversation languished for a few seconds.

Suddenly Torcuato burst out, 'I'll bet it's ten-twenty.'

Everyone looked at him in surprise.

'I'll bet,' insisted Torcuato.

'Why?' asked Pedro Salgado.

'Because they say that every twenty minutes an angel passes over and that's why people stop talking.'

'Well you're right. It is ten-twenty.'

Torcuato smiled triumphantly. 'You see?' he said.

Another angel passed over them, because they fell silent again. Ranulfo Quirarte – Old Friendly – watched the angel in its flight until it disappeared, and then said straight out, 'I know who killed the girl.'

'And how do you know?' asked Marcelino Huitrón.

Old Friendly pondered his answer for two swallows of beer.

'Because a little while ago, when we were talking about the safflower, I remembered that last night I was out with my lamp on Ethiel's land and since there weren't any deer I rode over to the fields by the river . . .'

Old Friendly stopped in mid-sentence to take another pull at his bottle. He wiped the foam from his mustache with the back of his hand and continued, 'I was riding with the lamp off when I heard someone on the path. I turned on the spotlight and about fifty meters away I saw some guy with his hands on a woman with a torn blouse . . .'

He broke off again. He rarely had such a captive audience and wasn't about to waste it.

'I'm out of beer,' he said to Ramón; 'pass me another.'

Ramón went into the store and brought one from the cooler. He wiped it with a rag, opened it and handed it over. Ranulfo continued his story.

'I think I scared them because they ran off into the dark. When I saw they'd dived into the huisache, I turned off the lamp 'cause I thought, Why the hell should I stick my nose where it doesn't belong? and you'll agree it's the wrong thing to do, right?'

Justino, whom Old Friendly had been addressing, nodded and the rest followed suit.

Ranulfo went on, 'And though I wasn't sticking my nose in, I clearly saw it was the Gypsy.' Again Old Friendly interrupted his story, knowing that no one would take over or change the subject, as would have happened on other occasions. He drank again, savoring the beer and proceeded:

'Last night I couldn't tell who was with him. It's just now that it hit me; it was the dead girl.'

Justino kept his eyes on him, questioningly. 'You're sure you're not making this up?'

Ranulfo kissed thumb and index finger in the shape of a cross. 'As God is my witness.'

'And about what time was that?' asked Marcelino.

'About four or five in the morning,' answered Old Friendly immediately.

Suddenly Lucio Estrada slapped his forehead. 'Now that I think of it,' he said, 'that goddam Gypsy was always admiring my knife . . . I'm sure he snatched it.'

Excited, Torcuato intervened. 'That's the son of a bitch who killed her. If not, he'd be here, cool as ever, talking to us, and I haven't seen him since yesterday.'

For the rest of the night, cold beer inflamed the heads of those men.

CHAPTER VIII

Gabriela Bautista

1

Night. The heat seems unrelenting. As does the dust. Heat and dust anoint people's bodies. Their skin exudes earth. Swarms of gnats and mosquitoes float in the motionless, searing air. They buzz in the ear, stinging implacably. A trio of coyotes howls on the hillside. Rattlesnakes slither along the burning gravel of the footpaths. Cattle crowd against the mesquites, taking shelter from a sun that burns even in the dark. In the distance, the river growls softly. And the heat, the damned heat, overcoming everything.

Gabriela Bautista cannot sleep; her nerves will not let her. Nor will her fear. Tensely she awaits the moment when her husband will return to beat her mercilessly and probably kill her. She has nowhere to flee, nowhere to hide. She holds on to the shadow of hope that he will not know; but no; by this time, he must have discovered her infidelity. If he is late, it is because he has gone to get even with the Gypsy for the affront.

The door creaks. Gabriela Bautista crouches behind the bed. It is he, and he will kill her. Another minute passes slowly. And then another. There is no repetition of the creak. Gabriela Bautista rests her head on the bed and closes her eyes. She oozes perspiration from her very depths. The same that ran through her the night before when a brutal shaft of light found her rubbing her flesh against the Gypsy's. A nameless light, insistent, silent, blinding them in the night, examining their nakedness.

'Good night,' yelled the Gypsy at the wordless shaft of light.

There was no answer, only silence and the light.

Gabriela Bautista hid behind the Gypsy and perspired, sweating fear.

'Good night,' repeated the Gypsy.

Nothing; light and silence; the cold fear of being silently hunted. In the dark, the Gypsy caught the glint of a rifle barrel. He pushed Gabriela towards the hill and both broke into a run with the shaft of light after them and an unknown pursuer behind them. They ran as long as they could, stumbling, burning their feet in the underbrush, scratching arms and legs, till the light ceased to penetrate the dense tangle of brush and branches. They curled up under the leaves of a hat-thorn acacia, panting, choking on the hot night air. Not a word passed between them. She nestled on top of him and he kissed her and caressed her and Gabriela Bautista let herself be kissed and caressed and kissed and caressed, growing more and more frightened of herself.

They made love. When he finished, the Gypsy stood up, buttoned his pants and walked away amid the huisache. Gabriela remained still, smeared with sex and fear. She heard the distant rumble of the Gypsy's pick-up as it departed along the dirt road. She listened as it disappeared into the dawn. She stood up, dusted and straightened her clothes, and began to walk awkwardly. They had been discovered and she had no idea where to run. She reached her house and hid in the only place she thought might give her cover: behind the bed, where she remained for the rest of that Sunday and from where she now hears the creaking of the door. She watches it open and sees her husband, Pedro Salgado, come in.

2

He drove as far as the dam and stopped his pick-up at the side of the road. He turned the motor off and stretched out on the seat. Again he savored Gabriela Bautista's kisses one by one. The woman drove him crazy and he her, but he knew he could not return to Loma Grande for a good while. He would have to wait for news and refrain from going back until he was sure there had been no clamor in the village.

He got out of the truck and walked to the edge of the reservoir. His ankles, forehead, forearms and hands were badly scratched. He removed his clothes, made a bundle and hid it under some bushes. Slipping into the tepid water, he rubbed himself with mud to disinfect the scratches and soothe the itch. A flock of green-winged teal flew low overhead, and the swish of their wings startled him, making him jump backwards. 'Shit,' he thought, 'I'm still nervous from last night's chase.'

He rinsed off the crust of mud, and splashed about, amusing himself for a while, trying to catch minnows with his hands. Out of the water, he dried himself with his shirt and put on his pants. He had no wish to remain naked, as it was early Sunday and sometimes cars with families traveled that road. Resting against one of the huge rocks set into the dam, he fell asleep.

Hardly anyone knew his name: José Echeverri-Berriozábal. Most everyone simply called him the Gypsy. He had been born in Tampico, the casual child of a Basque seaman and a waitress at the Elite ice-cream parlor. He inherited his stature and green eyes from his father. From his mother, broad bones, a slim and muscular build, and a precise control of adversity.

Since adolescence, he had developed the habit of getting involved with married women. He never discovered a reason for the preference, but his friends justified it by the fact that his mother had never married. At fifteen, an enraged husband had sliced him up with a machete. The Gypsy had barely survived the five gashes in his back. They had healed and he had worn the scars with pride ever since.

Three years later, it was the wife of a customs inspector. The man had caught them in bed and fired three 32-caliber slugs into his chest from a Browning automatic.

After he got over them, he swore vengeance. He found out that his attacker was lying up in Tempoal, and went to look for him without success, but fell in with a traveling salesman, who broke him in to the business of selling household items. From then on, he had rolled from one village to the next under the nickname 'the Gypsy.'

In time, he discovered the advantage of adding contraband Taiwanese electronics to his stock. If a frying pan doubled his profits, a quartz watch sextupled them. Even when he had to share his booty with rural, undercover state and federal police, mayors, and ejido delegates, he always came out ahead.

With his savings, he bought a Dodge pick-up with an aluminum cab and built himself a little house in Tampico. Even so, he never maintained a permanent residence, spending the night in his pick-up off dirt roads, or exchanging merchandise for a roof and a meal. He usually visited Loma Grande twice a year, until one January afternoon he began his affair with Gabriela Bautista. From then on, he increased the frequency of his visits to one a month.

In Loma Grande, he stayed at the home of Rutilio Buenaventura, an aged, blind campesino who had discovered a new way to lighten the darkness in which he lived, thanks to a Walkman the Gypsy had given him. In gratitude, Rutilio offered him his roof and his friendship, food being out of the question since he barely survived on the product of a dozen hens. They had become such close friends that only the old man knew why the Gypsy was so eager to come back to Loma Grande.

3

The lies, not the beers, were what finally intoxicated Ranulfo Quirarte – Old Friendly. He had invented the business of the Gypsy and Adela to take over the conversation, to titillate the curiosity of his hearers, so that he could put the finishing touches to his gossip as he pleased. His lies had submerged him in a hopeless orgy of drunken falsehoods from which he was neither able nor willing to extricate himself. His lies turned out to be so inebriating that he believed them himself. The other story – what had really happened – meant nothing. Only his story was now valid.

Only he knew that he had not been hunting by lamplight among the pastures along the river, but on the other side, in the huisache-covered fields leading to the slopes of El Bernal. Only he knew that the semi-nude torso, the bare breasts and the frightened face he had lit up that night belonged to Gabriela Bautista and not to the girl who had been knifed through the heart. Only he knew that the couple he had seen in the rays of his lamp were a pair of adulterers slaking their lust, not a murderer wrestling with his victim. Only he and no one else knew that.

Ranulfo realized that the hoax he had unleashed would become more ferocious and more dangerous, and that there was no longer any way to hold it back. He had intoxicated the other men in the village with his lies, and to all of them the Gypsy was guilty. This was the new truth and Ranulfo would have to believe it for ever.

4

The Gypsy felt a scorpion crawling over his ribs and slapped his chest hard, only to discover a slithering drop of sweat was what had really woken him up. He opened his eyes more than once to shake the sleep from them. Finally awake, it took him several seconds to recognize his surroundings, until the lapping of water against stones reminded him. He raised his head to see the sun reflected in a pool of perspiration gathered on his stomach. He stood up awkwardly, trying to put as little weight as possible on his numb left leg. A faint breeze blew across the reservoir and he shook his head to dry the perspiration dampening the nape of his neck. Looking up at the sky, he figured it was after noon. He had slept at least five hours, time enough with his face to the sun for his lips to be parched. He wet them with saliva and rubbed saliva into his stinging eyelids as well. Then he kneaded his thigh to get rid of the prickling numbness. While he massaged it, he tried to remember a dream, but none came to mind. And Gabriela Bautista's kisses were still so fresh on his tongue that he assumed he had dreamt of her.

Removing his pants, he took a running dive into the reservoir. The water, though lukewarm, provided some relief from the heat that was beginning to exasperate him. He floated face up, watching the loons fly across the water.

He amused himself in the reservoir until he felt hungry and then, getting out of the water, stood on a stone to dry himself in the sunlight. In the distance he could hear tractors turning earth over in a field. He enjoyed the sound, which reminded him of tugs maneuvering ships at the entrance to the port of Tampico.

He dressed and walked to the pick-up. Opening the door on the driver's side, he switched the radio on and scanned for a station, stopping at one that broadcast from Tampico, one he remembered from childhood. He turned up the volume and walked around to the back of the truck. Rummaging in a box he found a can of tuna, another of peas and a jar of mayonnaise, some chiles and a loaf of bread. He wolfed a sandwich made with four slices of bread, took the cap off a grapefruit Squeeze and climbed onto the hood to drink it. The station was broadcasting its 'Heartbreak Hour'. It occurred to him that real men were never left by a woman, and that the 'heartbroken' were a bunch of jerks, incapable of understanding a woman's desires. The announcer, who was of the opposite opinion, never stopped praising that 'class of noble and generous men who, no matter how they suffer, let their women go their own way'.

While the announcer preached 'the exquisite pain of lost love', the Gypsy recalled the previous night. Every night with Gabriela was more intense, and every intense night Gabriela felt more guilty and begged the Gypsy to leave her in peace; and he left Loma Grande and left Gabriela Bautista in peace, tangled in her peace, choking on her peace, avidly awaiting the night the Gypsy would return and tear it away from her.

'It is two-fifty p.m. and here is "I won't go near that gal again" by the Rio Grande Hurricanes,' oozed the announcer.

The Gypsy jumped off the hood, drank the rest of his soda and took the wheel. It was later than he thought. He had to drive to San Fernando to pick up a load of smuggled tape recorders. If he didn't hurry, he would arrive after nightfall and no longer find the dealer. It would then be hard to make the contact again.

He switched the radio off and the motor on. As he turned the wheel to the right, he suddenly stopped. Gabriela's kisses had not yet dissolved in his mouth. No woman had ever turned him on to that extent; he thought of her daily and often, her flesh calling him to her.

Slowly he turned the wheel to the left, towards the road which, in a straight line, entered Loma Grande's main street. As he accelerated, his mind was only on making off with Gabriela Bautista and holing up with her in Tampico. He gunned the pick-up decisively; after no more than a kilometer he suddenly braked to a stop. He looked fixedly at the horizon, took a deep breath, shifted into reverse and, turning the pick-up around, went back the way he had come.

5

Pedro Salgado slipped through the door into his house. Gabriela Bautista watched him intently, sheer terror

53

straining her eyes. Her husband was a man capable of slow brutality and she knew it. If he was going to kill her, it would be without fuss or excitement. Like the time when a single discrete motion with a scythe slashed the throat of a boy from another village who could not stop looking hungrily at Gabriela, and who survived thanks to the miracle performed by a rural doctor who, lacking surgical instruments, had sewn him up with a fishhook. No, there was no remorse in Pedro Salgado; he had demonstrated it on that and many other occasions. Even so, Gabriela considered him a good husband: affectionate, hard-working, responsible, and drunk only on weekends. He had never laid a hand on her, even though he had threatened to cut her to pieces if he ever discovered her to be unfaithful, a threat she knew he would fulfill to the letter.

Pedro saw his wife kneeling behind the bed and let loose a loud 'What the hell are you doing there?', which Gabriela interpreted as the preamble to a savage beating.

'I'm looking for my socks,' she managed to answer.

'And have you found them?'

All Gabriela could answer was a faint 'No'.

Pedro walked to the table and sat on a wooden bench.

'Make me some eggs and coffee, I'm hungry.'

Gabriela looked fearfully at Pedro, got up, poured the coffee into a cup and handed it to him. Pedro sweetened it with four spoons of sugar and began to drink slowly.

'Where were you all day?' he asked flatly.

Gabriela spilled cooking oil from the bottle in her hand and turned to her husband. She looked for a trace of restrained fury in his eyes, but found only the dullness of a two-day, non-stop binge. With eyebrows raised and mouth open, Pedro waited for the answer.

'I haven't left the house since last night,' said Gabriela with a poise inspired out of nowhere.

Pedro looked his wife up and down.

'Then you don't know?' he asked with a note of disbelief.

Gabriela again felt afraid. She could not tell if Pedro was leading her into a lie, or really asking her in all innocence. The doubt terrified her.

'Know what?' she asked unsteadily.

Had Pedro been sober he would have noticed his wife's nerves immediately, but his languid alcoholic stupor allowed for nothing more than: 'Somebody killed my cousin Ramón's girlfriend.'

Gabriela felt her fear dissipate little by little, so that she could speak without a tremor in her voice: 'Which Ramón? The one with the store?'

Pedro nodded. Relieved, Gabriela turned her back and began to cook the eggs. Pedro was so tired he began to sag onto the table until he was almost lying on it. Gabriela finished frying the eggs, put them on a plate and the plate in front of her husband. The aroma made him rub his face with both hands to wake himself up.

'Give me a roll,' he said.

Gabriela took one from a bag and handed it to him. Pedro broke it up and popped the yolk with one of the pieces. Gabriela noticed that he was wearing only a T-shirt.

'What happened to your shirt?'

Pedro's hand with the piece of bread stopped halfway to his mouth.

'I lent it to my cousin,' he answered after a pause. 'He needed one for the wake.'

'What was her name?' asked Gabriela innocently.

'Adela,' answered Pedro.

Gabriela pondered the name. 'Adela?'

'Yeah, but you wouldn't know her. She was one of the newcomers.'

'No, I didn't know her.'

Pedro returned to dipping bread into the yolk and eating it with evident gusto.

Gabriela watched every movement in search of a sign of hidden jealousy, but found none. Completely calm, she asked the last question: 'Do they know who killed her?'

Pedro downed a mouthful of coffee so that he could answer promptly and sputtered: 'Yes . . . the Gypsy . . .'

Gabriela Bautista was stunned and again felt herself sweating inside.

CHAPTER IX

Other People's Night

1

Astrid Monge was unable to shake the chill from her eyes for the rest of the night, nor rid them of the silhouette of her friend's corpse. She wanted no supper, upset by the odor of rancid leather that spilled from Adela. Seeing her so upset, her mother tried to give her some relief by applying nightshade compresses to her temples. They were useless: her daughter was overcome by the acid sensation of death.

Adela disappeared from one moment to the next and Astrid, had she not dressed her and felt her turning cold under her hands, would still not have believed it. Adela's death created a hole in her life. Even though they had known each other for a short time, a complicitous friendship had taken hold of them. They told each other things that neither imagined they could talk about among women. It was Astrid who had begun the exchange of confidences, talking about what she considered most intimate: rebellious dreams, unexpected desires. Soon, her trivial adolescent secrets were surpassed by Adela's insatiable stories. With her reserved manners of a reticent outsider, she was able to conceal the hot blood coursing through her veins. Little by little she had revealed the amorous desires eating away at her to Astrid, though never the name of the one who left the marks of what she called 'traces of passion' on her body: scratches, bites, purple circles beneath her nipples, in the folds of her abdomen, between her thighs, on the nape of her neck, hidden by her hair – all of which Astrid contemplated in amazement when Adela showed them to her with the pride of a satisfied female.

'I'm in love. Helplessly in love,' repeated Adela, time after time, without giving away the identity of her lover. It had taken Astrid a while to realize that Adela was involved with a married man with whom she curled up every day just before dawn, in the thick vegetation along the river bank.

Adela's parents had guessed at their daughter's romance. It was evident not only in her changes of mood and a lively joy, but because her mother often read the letters Adela wrote to her lover and innocently hid under the mattress on her cot. Devout Catholics who warned their children of the dangers and evils of sin, they never suspected the delighted orgasms with which Adela began her early mornings. The letters gave no hint of such a possibility. Written in a confused style, they seemed to refer to a relationship with a formal and straightforward boyfriend whose identity their daughter was hiding.

One night they decided to question her about the reasons for her secrecy. Adela answered their questions with composure, telling them that her boyfriend was from the village, of her own age, that he respected her completely, that his intentions were serious and that she would introduce him to them the very Sunday she was killed.

To sidestep the mess into which she had gotten herself, Adela had decided to ask Astrid's brother to act as her boyfriend for a couple of days. Whether out of prudence, embarrassment or shame, she could not bring herself to do it.

Her parents had swallowed Adela's fairy tale. Only Astrid shared with her the secrets of her wild love story and was the only one who knew that Adela was planning to run away with her nameless lover to the nameless wastes of the Tamaulipas Sierra. She did not insist on finding out the name, losing interest in it, in the face of Adela's stubborn refusal to reveal it. Her curiosity had not returned until the moment she heard of the murder and a string of possibilities crossed her mind. One by one, she discarded them all. None of them fitted the description Adela gave her of her man. The fact was that Adela had not described him with such basic adjectives as tall, light-skinned, handsome, swarthy, slim, heavy, but with far more substantial ones: rough, tough and a great lay – three qualities that would be hard for just any man to merit.

Astrid supposed that Ramón Castaños must have been the one who finally supplied Adela with her alibi. He fitted the description of the timid boyfriend she had sketched. Evidently her parents had fallen for the ploy and that was why they were so attentive to him, treating him as if he were one of the closest mourners.

Astrid stopped her mental pursuit of suspects when her brother came home in the early morning. He had come back from the store bearing the urgent news that the Gypsy had murdered Adela. For a moment, Astrid was confused. She couldn't see the Gypsy as her friend's possible lover and therefore her most likely killer. The Gypsy was neither married, nor lived in Loma Grande, and Adela always bragged that her man made love to her every day. But it surely must be he, the only one around who fitted the fleeting portrait Adela had painted.

The widow Castaños tried to move as little as possible, to prevent those outside from noticing the creaking of the rocking chair she had pulled up to the wall so that she could hear the conversation on the other side. Most of what she heard that Sunday night repeated the Gypsy's guilt, until one sentence stood out among the rest in that beery atmosphere: 'You have to avenge her . . . kill him,' declared a blurred voice, belonging to Torcuato Garduño. The widow figured it was directed at her son and put her ear to the crack through which she was peeping.

First she heard Ramón's silence and then a chorus of laughter. At first she couldn't guess what was happening but inferred that Torcuato was joking and that the others were making fun of Ramón's pallor. She was right; it seemed impossible that Ramón would have the courage to take on the Gypsy. Ramón knew it and so did the others, for the simple reason that few, if any of them, had it either. By showing off his eight mortal scars, the five machete slashes and the three bullet holes, the Gypsy had created a myth of invulnerability. 'He has a double-thick skin,' it was said; 'that's why he can take so much.' Further vague and remote rumors credited him with the deaths of four men. But, above all, Loma Grande was, in the final analysis, a law-abiding village where no one had taken justice into his own hands for a long time.

'Carmelo Lozano will take care of that bastard,' declared Justino Téllez.

The widow Castaños heard the murmured approval of the listeners. She was pleased, not wanting to see her son mixed up in a lost cause. She had pulled her ear away from the crack, satisfied with Justino's solution, when

Marcelino Huitrón's grave voice brought it back to the wall.

'Don't be a wimp,' he growled at Ramón; 'you kill that son of a bitch, because Carmelo Lozano won't lay a finger on him.'

This time there was neither laughter nor jokes. Marcelino's son had been run over and Carmelo had let the driver go in exchange for a thousand-peso bribe. He had kept him locked up for barely half a day.

'Carmelo and that son of a bitch are partners,' insisted Marcelino, which was true. The Gypsy paid the police commander a monthly retainer so that he could smuggle contraband into southern Tamaulipas.

'He won't do a thing to him,' he repeated; 'Lozano won't wring the neck of one of his own chickens.'

Justino Téllez tried to interrupt. He had always argued that crimes should not be resolved by violence. He had witnessed the feud between the Jiménez and Duarte families and knew that vengeance never pacified such enmity – quite the contrary. Both families had been exterminated without ever solving their differences. He was convinced that jail was better than bloodshed.

When Téllez tried to speak, Marcelino shut him up.

'Don't start whining, Justino,' he said, shoving his face into the other's. 'Some things have to be put right between machos.'

He turned his back on Téllez and stared at Ramón. 'And if you're not man enough to kill him, I will,' he said without hesitating.

'Don't get all worked up, Lino; this is none of your business,' broke in Justino Téllez, 'and if it's a man's job, let Ramón take care of it his way.'

Marcelino nodded his head heavily. 'OK,' he said, 'I'll

shut up. I just have one more question.' The others eyed him expectantly. Marcelino was staring at Ramón again. 'So, what the fuck are you going to do?' he asked straight out. There was a deep silence. From her rocking chair, the widow wanted to scream 'Leave my boy alone,' but was just able to murmur an inaudible 'Lord save us.'

Ramón's stomach palpitated at the question. He had no way out. There was only one answer to that question. He swallowed hard: either he was a man for ever or would never be one again.

'I'll kill him,' he answered, the bile burning his throat; 'I'll kill him as soon as I see him.'

Marcelino raised the beer bottle in his hand. 'Salud,' he mumbled.

Justino Téllez patted Ramón on the shoulder. 'That's it,' he said.

Blood had won out and he would do nothing to stop it flowing. Ramón would have to take care of it himself.

3

A mouse flashed across the table, grabbed a piece of tortilla from a dirty plate and fled over the bench. Natalio Figueroa watched it all the way into a crack under the wardrobe. It was 3 a.m. and Natalio was waiting for the news that might identify his daughter's killer.

As a child, his mother had told him that bad news came at night. By now Natalio had discarded that statement. He had received all his bad news in broad daylight: at eleven o'clock of a Sunday morning in June he had been advised that his son Erasmo was gasping his last, stretched out in a muddy street with his skull holed by a random shot fired by a mindless drunk celebrating the end of an all-night binge with aimless gunfire; at eight o'clock of a Saturday morning in April the news had reached his front door that his son Marcos had been thrown into a pile of rock from the back of a spooked horse, pulverizing the fragile string of bones connecting his neck to his head; and yesterday, at three in the afternoon, just to corroborate the fact that bad news came in daylight, Evelia had informed them that their daughter's body lay like a discarded rag at the edge of a sorghum field.

He took a sip of cold, watery coffee. His wife lay drowsily mumbling nightmares. Natalio watched her without emotion. He no longer had the strength to console her, nor the desire to live. His only comfort was the chance to know the identity of the murderer, so that he could shove a knife into his chest.

Natalio perceived a barely audible but incessant tapping in the room. He peered at the table and found a moth frantically beating its wings against the cover of an enameled pot. Natalio picked it up between finger and thumb, pulled off its wings and dropped it. The moth staggered a few centimeters over the floor and was lost in the shadows.

Natalio blew away the dust its wings had left on his fingers. The neighbor's dogs began barking. Natalio stood up and looked out the window. In the dark, he could not see who was approaching, but assumed that someone was coming to tell him about the murderer.

He stood behind the door, expecting a knock, and nervously awakened Clotilde with a whistle. Alarmed, the woman sat up on the bed.

'What is it?' she asked dully, still half asleep.

Natalio pointed to the door. Without understanding what was going on, his wife put on her scuffs and joined him.

'Good evening,' said a voice on the other side of the door. Natalio opened the door and found himself face to face with two strangers he could not remember having seen at the funeral. He examined them before responding.

'Evening,' he said shortly.

One of the men held up a plastic bag and offered it to him. 'We've brought you some supper.'

The visitors' unexpected cordiality upset him. He took the bag, whispering his thanks, then stood in silence, as did the other two. From inside the house Clotilde asked them in.

'Wouldn't you like a cup of coffee?' she asked.

The two men came in and sat down at the table. Clotilde opened the bag and emptied its contents onto a platter: six tacos of scrambled eggs with potatoes and onions. Not in the least bit hungry, Natalio forced himself to eat one for the sake of appearances. The rest were devoured by the strangers, on the pretext of filling their stomachs to counteract the effects of all the beer they had been drinking.

Neither mentioned the crime. They spent their time talking to each other about how many sheep they had lost to coyotes, the dates of the next dances to be held at Xico, the elections for a new ejido delegate and the level of the reservoir during the dry season. It was as if they had come to Natalio's house for no other reason than to continue an ongoing conversation.

Clotilde and Natalio listened patiently for an hour and a half, until one of the strangers decided it was time to go. Discouraged by the lack of information about the murderer in their dialogue, Natalio stood up to see them off.

'Night,' he said to them.

'G'night,' answered the more cordial of the two as he stood staring at Natalio.

'What's the matter?' asked Natalio anxiously.

The other held back his answer for a moment or two.

'Nothing. We only wanted to tell you that we know who killed your little girl.'

Natalio shivered: 'Who?' he asked, trying to control his agitation.

'A guy they call the Gypsy . . .'

Seeing that Natalio showed no signs of recognition, the man added: 'The one who drives a black Dodge.'

Fury shook Natalio's temples; he had no idea who they were talking about, but he would go and find him. All they had to do was tell him which way to go.

'Where does he live?'

The man smacked his lips. 'You won't find him around here . . . he's not from these parts.'

'He's a mean son of a bitch, that Gypsy,' added the other man. 'He has debts pending in several settlements.'

'Well I'm going to collect this one,' declared Natalio, 'because I'm going to kill the son of a bitch.'

The man shook his head.

'No what?' asked Natalio, stung.

'You've already been beaten out,' answered the man, 'because a little while ago the guy who swore he would do it was Ramón Castaños.'

'He has no obligation,' declared Natalio.

The man shook his head again. 'The boy's already sworn and he'll look bad if he doesn't keep his word . . .

Besides he is obliged because he was going to marry your daughter.'

The answer calmed the old man. If Ramón had committed to avenging Adela, he had to respect his decision.

'The Gypsy took off right after,' added the man, 'but Ramón promised to get him.'

'I'll look him up after it's done, to give him my thanks,' said Natalio.

4

The first time the Gypsy had embraced her, Gabriela Bautista felt fear, not for what he had done to her, but for what she herself felt. The man had grabbed her around the waist, taking her by surprise, as she returned from feeding the goats in the corral behind her house. She had tried to get loose. Pedro, her husband, would soon be back in the truck that brought the cotton-pickers from the plantations at El Salado. The Gypsy had immobilized her with words, not force.

'I'll let you go if you want me to,' he said.

She stopped struggling. Their glances had met often enough for them both to understand that his embrace was no accident. Nevertheless, the place and the hour made his move untimely and dangerous. Gabriela had no desire to separate herself from the man who was holding her tightly, but she had no intention of causing a calamity. She found no better way to calm him, without rejecting him, than to go limp and roll her eyes skyward.

The Gypsy was at a loss to interpret the woman's pliancy as she slid from his arms. He reacted by tightening his grip. There was no change in her lack of resistance.

Disappointed, he let her go, without realizing that beneath her coldness, Gabriela was hiding a desire that choked her.

'I'd better leave,' murmured the Gypsy, half annoyed, half embarrassed.

With no change of expression, Gabriela said: 'Don't let me go.'

Confused, the Gypsy turned and kissed her mouth. Automatically, Gabriela raised her hands and grasped the man's torso. Under his shirt, soaked with perspiration, she could feel the rippled scars covering his back. She became even more excited. His furrowed back felt overpoweringly virile. She tensed, licked his bitter mouth and pushed him away.

'Go away,' she commanded.

Excited, the Gypsy tried to embrace her again, but Gabriela elbowed him away.

'Get out of here,' she repeated; 'Pedro will be here any minute . . . come for me some other time.'

The Gypsy left, satisfied Gabriela would not get away from him again. She remained standing in the middle of the lot, feeling humid heat unleashed between her legs.

That night she had not been able to stop thinking of his scar-furrowed back, just as she was unable to stop thinking of it two years later, the night Pedro revealed to her that the Gypsy had murdered Adela Figueroa. Only this time she imagined it differently, not as the back that had trembled with passion on top of her, but as the back of a man who would be pursued until they had killed him. That was her nightmare: that they would cut him down from the back, since it would be the only way they could kill him. No one would dare to meet him face to face.

There was no way the Gypsy could have committed the crime of which he was accused. Only she knew that, for sure, and only she could prove his innocence. But to confess the truth would expose herself to exchanging her life for his. She was afraid and thought there was nothing she could do to save him, nothing at all. She curled up in the sheets and sobbed. She remembered his back again, the hours they had spent together and the tremendous desire to be with him. She had never thought her secret would be so painful. She closed her eyes and tried to sleep in the clamminess of the night.

5

Justino Téllez tossed and turned on his bed and opened his eyes again. His head was spinning – not from the countless splits of Victoria beer he had drunk, not from hours of insomnia during a night soaked in mosquitoes and humid heat, not from so much involvement with the murder, but from a vague idea stuck in his conscience which kept him from sleeping.

He had no reason to be so concerned. The crime had been solved. Besides Ranulfo Quirarte's testimony, there had been other versions of the Gypsy's behavior confirming his guilt. Torcuato Garduño remembered seeing him hanging around Adela's house several times in the early morning. Macedonio Macedo declared he had seen him sharpening a knife identical to the one stolen from Lucio Estrada. Pascual Ortega reported the lewd compliments the Gypsy aimed at Adela, to which she had responded with utter indifference. Juan Carrera heard him talk about the tremendous jealousy he felt for a woman in the village with whom he said he was in love and whose name he never mentioned, and Pedro Salgado had noticed the

Gypsy behaving strangely for some time. Everything pointed to the Gypsy as the killer.

It was almost nine in the morning and Justino, who had dropped on his bed at five, still couldn't sleep. Something didn't fit, a vague detail that was out of place, that pricked his insomnia and that Justino, befuddled by the alcohol he had consumed, was unable to place.

He thrashed about between his sheets for a long time, trying unsuccessfully to doze off. 'Shit,' he thought, 'what the hell is wrong with me?' A bitter taste burned his throat and tongue. He was on the verge of collapse from exhaustion, but the damned idea that left him sleepless refused to take shape. If his wife had been alive, she would have prescribed a remedy for his condition, but he was a widower and there was no one in the house to advise him.

He got up disjointedly and staggered over to a basket he used as a pantry. Fumbling around in search of something that would calm him down, he pulled out a jar of instant coffee, a can of powdered milk, some packaged tamales, a piece of dried horse meat, tomatoes, green chiles, until he finally found what he needed: ebony seeds.

He put them on the stove to boil. When the water began to turn reddish, he removed the pan and added two spoons of powdered milk. He drank the infusion bit by bit until there was none left, and then returned to the bed. The potion took effect and Justino began to doze. The idea hammering at his brain, though still confused, came to mind from time to time, but no longer made any difference; drowsiness was overtaking him.

He was almost asleep when suddenly an image that made everything clear took shape: a footprint one span and three fingers long, the murderer's footprint. The

Gypsy's foot measured at least two fingers more. That was what was spinning around in his head and the last thing that came to mind before he fell into a deep sleep.

CHAPTER X

Love Letters

1

Finally, after a long struggle, Ramón Castaños came up
with the exact word to express the chaos piling up inside
him since the previous day.

'Check,' he murmured.

Torcuato Garduño and Jacinto Cruz, each lost in his
own drunken monologue, raised their heads at the same
time.

'Wha . . . ?' asked Torcuato, slurring the vowel.

'Nothing,' answered Ramón.

The others looked at him with glassy eyes and went
back to their mumbling. Ramón repeated to himself:
'Check,' this time in such a quiet whisper that no one
heard him.

He had no real idea of what 'check' meant; nevertheless,
he had read in a cowboy story that the hero, surrounded
by a tribe of Apaches, yelled to his buddies: 'They've got
us in check.' Ramón couldn't remember the end of the
plot, but he retained the word that expressed the dire situation of its characters, and from then on he used it for his
own troubles.

'I'm in check,' he thought gravely, imagining himself a
cowboy surrounded by Apaches. But he was much deeper
in check when, at seven in the morning, still standing
behind his counter, having had no sleep and being obliged
to put up with the stupidity of a pair of drunks, his psyche

perturbed by a love affair with a corpse he was obliged to avenge, he saw Natalio Figueroa approaching the store.

His attempt to take refuge beside the shelves and remain unnoticed so that the old man would pass him by was in vain, because at that hour of the morning Natalio was looking precisely for him.

The old man reached the door of the shop and murmured a 'G'morning'. Torcuato and Jacinto turned and, recognizing him, rose clumsily to their feet. Ramón, whose swollen eyes testified to the all-night binge, responded to the greeting with a timid nod. Natalio Figueroa, his hands in his pockets, slumped on a chair and began to examine the shelves as if he were undecided about what to buy.

Torcuato and Jacinto sat down again. To Ramón, Natalio seemed more aged than the previous day, as if the old man would break in two at the slightest movement.

Ramón had no wish to talk to him or to anyone else; all he could think of was bed and sleep for three days without interruption.

'Have you had breakfast?' asked Natalio, intending to take him home for breakfast so that he could talk to him alone.

'Yes,' answered Ramón with assurance.

Torcuato Garduño stared at him dully. 'When did you do that? You've been here all night,' he dragged out with great effort.

Ramón pointed to some shelves loaded with packaged junk food. 'I've been snacking and I'm not hungry any more,' he lied, because in fact his stomach was growling. He had eaten only some corn chips and a couple of Twinkies, but he was anxious to get rid of Natalio and the two drunks as soon as possible. He didn't want to talk or stand

72

on his feet or go over Adela's death again. He had had enough.

Natalio realized that the boy was tired and fed up, but he badly needed to see him.

'My wife made some fish tamales and told me to invite you,' added Natalio, convinced that Ramón would not refuse such a direct proposal.

Ramón came around the counter, asked Torcuato and Jacinto to give up their chairs and put them in the back of the store along with the tables. Then he closed the door and tied a rope through the two rings. 'I'll be right back,' he shouted to his mother, said goodbye to the two night-owls with a 'See you later', and then 'OK, let's go', to the old man.

2

On the way to the Figueroa home, Ramón began to feel sick. Not only because he was going back to the room still bathed in the smell of Adela dead, but because at every step beside Natalio he imagined that it was Adela walking next to him. Both had the same look, similar gestures and even a similar gait. The cicadas were chirping and the sun broiling as they had the previous morning when he had touched Adela's tepid skin. It was thus that Adela materialized, step by step: smiling in her father's smile, breathing in his breath, walking in his steps. Ramón, who had never heard more than two sentences from her, heard her joking, crying, laughing. He stopped to rest in the middle of the street, closed his eyes and massaged the nape of his neck. Instead of disappearing, the spectral image of Adela grew within him. It grew so far as to make him turn a look of

73

desperation on the old man, who could only ask, 'What's the matter?' Natalio's grave voice broke the spell and Adela's shade collapsed into the dust of the morning.

'Nothing . . . nothing is the matter with me,' answered Ramón with a tremulous sigh.

Ramón walked into the house and smelled the familiar scent of roses that had been on Adela when he found her lying at the corner of the sorghum field. Clotilde Aranda had spread a few drops of the fragrance around to cover the traces of the corpse. The cloying floral aroma dizzied Ramón; Adela's specter had slipped into him through his nostrils. He glimpsed her again on the cot, naked, smelling of roses, raising her arms to him. 'It's a dream . . . I'm tired,' he thought and, resigned to suffering the dead girl's omnipresence a little while longer, he left Adela lying on the cot and sat down to breakfast.

Clotilde served the tamales with refried beans on the side and black coffee. Ramón ate swiftly, almost without raising his eyes from the plate. He was so absorbed in every mouthful that Natalio and Clotilde decided not to distract him, and munched their sorrow in silence. When they finished, Clotilde removed the plates, carefully cleaned the table, leaving nothing on it. Ceremoniously, Natalio stood up to get a cardboard box. He put it on his knees and took out a handful of papers from which he carefully withdrew one.

'These are Adela's marks from when she was in fifth grade,' he said. He handed the yellowing sheet to Ramón. 'She was good at studying . . . the teacher said she was the best in the school,' continued Natalio with a barely noticeable expression of pride.

Before looking at the multiple As and Bs in Spanish, Math, Social Sciences, Natural Sciences, Ramón looked at the photograph of Adela stapled to the top of the report card. It was a dull, wrinkled, black-and-white, three-quarter profile of the girl. She looked grave, her hair combed back, her forehead clear and her light-colored eyes focused in the distance.

'She was thirteen in that photo,' remarked Clotilde, 'and she was the tallest in her class.'

Ramón turned to face her, to ask a banal question, but the woman had stopped talking and paying attention to him. Something had crossed her mind, leaving a distant and childish grimace on her face. Ramón examined the picture again. Adela was not wearing earrings; nor was there any visible make-up on her lips or eyelashes. Around her neck hung a narrow chain lost in the folds of her blouse: a white blouse. Ramón wondered if the day she had been photographed she was wearing the yellow skirt. He could not imagine her dressed otherwise than she had been the afternoon he had met her.

Natalio searched the box and took out another photograph, one in faded, washed-out colors, in which Adela was sitting in the center of an iron bench with a bandstand in the background.

'This was the last picture taken of her,' said the old man, his voice cracking. 'It was a little before we moved here.'

'Where's that?' asked Ramón.

'That's the main square of León, on Adela's birthday,' answered Clotilde.

Ramón wanted to ask the date, but he didn't dare. Adela smiled from the photograph, and Ramón had never seen her smile. Nor did he know her birthday.

3

Ramón's morning was spent among photographs, locks of hair, report cards, broken dolls, Christmas cards and school medals. Clotilde and Natalio, more for themselves than for Ramón, were trying to recover their daughter amid these odds and ends.

At first, Ramón listened with interest; breakfast had raised his spirits. But by midday he began to feel overcome with fatigue. The old folks' stories bewildered him. Several times he asked for strong coffee, wanting to stave off the weight of his hangover and, at all costs, prevent Adela from materializing in her father's face. Three times he tried to leave, but the old couple wrapped his departure in endless memories, making it impossible. On his fourth attempt, determined to leave, Natalio held him back with a 'Wait a second.' He went to the wardrobe and returned with a bundle of letters, which he placed on the table.

'They're yours,' he said.

Embarrassed, Ramón looked at the letters.

'Mine, why?'

'Adela wrote them to you,' answered her father.

Ramón, who in his anxiety to be gone was already standing, sat down again. Clotilde intervened.

'Adela had already told us about you.'

Ramón's heart beat rapidly. There must be some mistake. He had really had nothing to do with her.

The woman picked up the bundle of letters and put it in his hands. 'Take them,' she insisted softly. 'They're love letters.'

Confused, Ramón tried to return them; but Clotilde rejected them firmly.

'My daughter loved you, don't reject her now that she's dead,' she said bitterly.

'They're yours,' repeated Natalio, noting the boy's reluctance. 'She used to write them to you at night, when she thought we were asleep.'

Ramón kept the bundle. Though he found it hard to believe them, he did not think they were trying to deceive him.

He said goodbye, but before he could depart Natalio stopped him.

'Thank you,' he said.

'What for?' asked Ramón hesitantly.

'For loving my daughter and sparing me the burden of killing a man.'

Ramón put as much distance as he could between himself and Loma Grande, running with long strides through the scrub with the letters under his arm. Looking for shade where he could sit peacefully and read them, he found a rock engulfed by the trunk of a mesquite. The letters, close to fifty of them, were in unsealed envelopes and all, without exception, were fragrant with attar of roses.

He began to leaf through them at random. Most of them were addressed to an anonymous 'My love'. The rest, not even that. Drawings of flowers and hearts with the legend 'You and I' headed the pages. Some of them were written in a careful studied hand, others scribbled with unintelligible corrections. The syntax was uneven and chaotic, a jungle of disconnected sentences. Ramón soon realized why. Adela had combined her own thoughts with the words of popular songs copied from the series of song books entitled *Notitas Musicales*. So much confusion suggested coded messages for a lover who might well be the Gypsy. And Ramón might have believed that, if he had not found five lines that erased all doubt from his mind:

Today I met you in the store. You are the man of my daybreak. I like you a lot. I'll return to the store a hundred times just to see you. I want to be the only one on the horizon of your love.

That paragraph was enough for Ramón to change the careless way he was reading the letters. From then on, he found any number of hidden references that coincided with the three times they had met face to face. In them, Adela alluded to details known only to the two of them. He no longer had the slightest doubt: Adela had secretly loved him. Now it was his turn to return that love.

4

Clotilde Aranda and Natalio Figueroa awoke from the bottomless stupor of their siesta to a knocking at the door. Natalio pulled back the curtain to reveal Ramón's face at the window.

'What is it?' he asked.

Ramón leaned forward, the bundle of letters still in his hand. He was sweaty and looked upset.

'I've come to ask you a favor,' he said.

'What?'

He leaned closer, silhouetted against the sunlight and took a deep breath. 'Give me a picture of Adela.'

The old man, dazzled by the five-o'clock blaze behind Ramón, shook his head. 'The ones I showed you are all I have.'

'I know, but I don't have any,' objected Ramón.

78

Natalio hesitated. He had no wish to give up a single one of the eight photographs he still had of his daughter: they were the most vivid memento that remained of her. 'No,' he declared firmly.

Clotilde joined them, holding up the eight photos fan-wise in her hand, and Natalio turned to look at her reproachfully.

'I'll lend you one,' she said, heedless of her husband.

Ramón looked them over, one by one: Adela at three, in an old woman's lap; at five, with other kids; at ten, greeting her godfather; at eleven, at her first communion, and afterward outside the church with the priest and her parents; at fourteen, looking out the window of a bus; at fifteen, at a school ceremony; on her fifteenth birthday, sitting on a cast-iron bench. Natalio had told him the story of each one: where it was taken, by whom, the date, the circumstances.

Clotilde spread the fan. 'Choose,' she said.

Ramón looked them over again, from left to right and back.

'I don't want any of these.'

Clotilde shrugged. 'Then which?' she asked, confused. 'These are all we have.'

Still dazzled by the sun behind Ramón, they missed his gesture towards the box, which was still on the table.

'That one,' he said.

Clotilde looked around the room.

'Which one?' she asked, puzzled.

'The one on the report card.'

Clotilde went to get it, removed the staples carefully so as not to damage it, and handed it to Ramón, repeating, 'It's just a loan.'

'You have to bring it back,' added Natalio.

Ramón went home, greeted his mother with a laconic 'Hi', and dropped on his bed. Tired as he was, he reread all the letters. They were all undated, but he tried to put them into some chronological order, adding his own hearts in pencil; and, to dispel any doubt about who they were addressed to, endlessly filled in 'Ramón and Adela'. Taking the ID photo out of the left pocket of Pedro's borrowed shirt, he lay there admiring it for a long time. He forgot for the moment that Adela was no more than inert flesh underground. He forgot because he could see her seated next to him on the bed, her hair pulled back, caressing him with a smile. He forgot because he was sound asleep and dreaming.

CHAPTER XI

One Span and Three Fingers

1

Justino Téllez woke up, startled by the thunder of one of his own snores.

'Who's there?' he shouted.

He rose and meticulously searched the whole room. Finding no one, he decided it must have been a cat. When he ran his fingers through his hair, they came away wet. The whole house was impregnated with a palpable greasy heat, like oil in the air.

'Shit!' he murmured.

He had slept in his clothes, as he always did, and, as always, he swore at the stench of old age it left on him. Taking off his shirt, he soaked a sponge in a basin of water and freshened his arms, neck and armpits. He wanted to change his gray, sodden undershirt, but the others he had were dirtier yet. He decided to leave it on: nobody cared what he wore any more, anyway.

He spat out the sour taste of a long night and stale beer, gargled with tepid water and pushed the door open to air the room. Sunlight still reverberated furiously in the street. He looked at his watch.

'Four,' he confirmed, 'and no end to this fucking heat.'

He turned back to light the stove. The flame flickered uncertainly, indicating he was almost out of gas. He'd have to go to Mante soon, to exchange the tank. He put a frying pan on the burner containing leftovers of armadillo crackling, a present from his compadre Hector Montonaro. He let it sizzle for several minutes, in anticipation of the bitter taste of almost carbonized meat.

He ate slowly, the more to enjoy it, sucking each little bone clean, then opened a lukewarm Coke and downed it without stopping. He remembered the murderer's footprints, thinking he'd have to return to the scene to measure them again. Then he'd look for Rutilio Buenaventura to ask if he knew the Gypsy's shoe size.

Justino left the house with a bag of scraps. Two skinny, mangy strays pranced up, wagging their tails; but when he threw them the scraps, they pounced, snarling at each other.

The afternoon waned as he followed the dirt track to the river, but not the heat, which seemed rooted in the dirt. A handful of male blackbirds perched in the branches of a mesquite squawked noisily. Jack rabbits flashed from among the nopal cactuses as he passed. He picked up a stone to throw at their heads before they took off, the way he had as a kid. He used to daze them with a stone and then break their necks with the edge of his palm. It had been a long time since he'd got one that way, but it didn't stop him trying, whenever he had the chance.

Reaching the sorghum field, he was overcome by the peace of the afternoon. Quail filled the stand with their song, and white-winged doves pecked at the ears of grain. He walked to the exact spot where Adela had fallen. All that was left of the crime was a brown patch of dried blood and stalks of sorghum cane flattened by the weight of the corpse. It looked like any other planted field, though not for long: Victor Vargas, who cultivated it, had sworn the previous night, before witnesses, never to plow it again. 'Because it will never stop reeking of death,' he explained.

82

The field was condemned to be swallowed by weeds and scrub; no one would rent it, or seek it as an abandoned land concession.

2

Justino scrutinized the area. Adela's and the murderer's footprints were still clearly visible. He squatted and measured them: a span for hers, a span and three fingers for the killer's. He repeated the procedure to make sure. Out of curiosity, he measured his own footprint: a span, three fingers and a bit. The killer probably wore size nine-and-a-half, as he did.

He followed the imprints to see where they came from. Sometimes he lost them, but he went around in circles until he found them again. The loose earth around the prints indicated that both of them had been running and that Adela had not stopped until she was killed. The trail led into a field of high, thickly matted grass, which Justino did not venture to cross. At that hour of the afternoon, this was the favored territory of the fer-de-lance, a pit viper that made his skin crawl. He had seen the effect of its venom on cattle. They bellowed uncontrollably, kicking furiously until they collapsed, strangled by their own spasms. He skirted the expanse of grass until he reached the river bank. Estimating the point at which he had left their trail and following imaginary coordinates, he examined the marshy banks of the river. All he found was deer and coati tracks, but by chance he discovered a narrow cattle path trampled through the brush bordering the river. He pushed his way into it with great difficulty, ducking continually to avoid being scratched by the lower stalks. Passage became almost impossible, but by the time he decided he was ready to give up and turn back, it was too late: he had covered more than two hundred meters; the way back was as daunting as the way forward. He decided to push on. At each step he raised clouds of mosquitoes, which riddled him with bites, though he squashed a few, flailing his arms and hands. Inside his green tunnel, the heat intensified brutally, humidity and mud coating his skin with slime. Sweat soaked his clothes and his back creaked with every step at half-crouch. 'What the fuck am I doing here?' he groaned out loud.

He kept on for another two hundred meters, practically on his hands and knees, before suddenly he burst into a huge clearing hidden by a stand of trees. Justino stumbled out of the crawlway and sat down to rest on an abandoned anthill, while a flock of brown jays screeched at his intrusion. He threw a lump of dirt to frighten them off and they headed towards the river, where they continued their ruckus.

In spite of his exhaustion, Justino decided on one last effort in his search to unravel the crime.

The area was unfamiliar to him, but everything pointed to the field of tall grass he had avoided, ending at this clearing. Only here, the grass was shorter and sparser, a natural pasture for the cattle that had discovered it. The looseness of the earth, because of its proximity to the river, recorded every mark; but the confusion of hoofprints made it well-nigh impossible to find the trail. He would have failed, had he not found, near a palm tree, a patch of grass cut down by machete, in the center of which lay, neatly folded by a white sheet, a black skirt and a blue blouse.

She had not been stripped with violence. Neither garment was torn or split. On the contrary, they were both carefully folded without a wrinkle or a stain. Under the blouse lay a pair of shoes, panties and a brassiere, and around them the couple's footprints. Justino examined them one by one. They came from the river bank and proved beyond doubt that killer and victim had arrived together, their footprints side by side. At intervals, they stopped tip to tip, as if the couple had kissed or embraced. At first the trail consisted of shoe prints: his in high-heeled western boots, hers in the shoes lying under the blouse. Then they were delinquently bare around the sheet. The rest was confusion: the man's footsteps back and forth, first bare, then shod, which finally led away, fifty steps westward. Adela's steps exploded from the sheet in frenzied flight, his behind hers, covering the fifty steps and throwing up mud at every stride. The chase continued towards the thick, high grass, and from there to the corner of the sorghum field where the ferocious pursuit was consummated.

Justino felt confused. He could not explain the murderer's sudden motivation to stick a knife into Adela, minutes after making love to her. Compliantly and tenderly, Adela had prepared for her own death. Her clothes carefully folded on the loving sheet, her dawn nudity in the secluded clearing, all convulsed in terrified flight and a knife to the heart. Why?

Justino picked up the rose-scented skirt and blouse, testimony to the fact that Adela was involved with her killer and had not been forcibly stripped. At the very least, they contradicted Ranulfo Quirarte's version that he had seen her with her blouse torn.

He opened his pocket knife and ripped the clothes and the sheet to shreds. With a palm frond, he obliterated his footsteps, then walked to the river and threw in the shreds of cloth and the shoes. What was left of the evidence swirled briefly in the current, amid leaves and stalks, and then sank below the surface, downstream.

To have taken it into the village would have been useless, changing no one's conviction that the Gypsy was the killer. The only outcome would have been the real killer trying to wipe out both the evidence and its finder. Nor was he about to show up with the news that Adela was an oversexed little girl with an itch, struck down with half an ejaculation still smeared on her corpse. Why mortify her parents? Best not embroil things more than they were and hope that the Gypsy, if he were really innocent, might never return to Loma Grande; and if he did, pray they didn't kill him.

It began to get dark. Justino left the clearing the same way the lovers had come to their final tryst. It was a faint trail, hard to follow, hidden by patches of spurge nettle and cat-claw, that met the dirt road leading from Loma Grande to Ejido Pastores.

Amid lengthening shadows, Justino took his bearings and headed south, toward Rutilio Buenaventura's house.

4

Rutilio was listening to a Tigres del Norte cassette on the Walkman the Gypsy had given him. Along with another of a fictitious interview with Caro Quintero, the drug lord in jail, it was one of his favorites. He had more than seventy.

The Gypsy brought him five or six every time he came to Loma Grande, buying them in gas stations or trailer stops. He tried to vary the selection: cumbias, mambos, rock, polkas, dirty jokes, even radio recordings of the best soccer games played by the Roadrunners of the University of Tamaulipas.

Rutilio relieved his endless afternoons of sightlessness listening to his Walkman. He had lost his eyesight eight years before and blamed it on the months he had worked in an insecticide warehouse. In any event, trachoma had left him in the dark. The infection had been so severe that the doctor who had taken care of him had removed both eyeballs and replaced them with two crude, inexpensive glass prostheses.

Justino saw the old man through a window slumped in a chair, with his headphones on, his eyelids shut, surrounded by a dozen or so chickens. Rutilio kept them in the house to protect them from raccoons and their ringtailed cat cousins. He survived on their eggs and the fifty dollars a month sent him by a daughter working in a 7-Eleven in Harlingen, Texas.

'G'afternoon,' yelled Justino from the window.

One of the hens flapped upward, squawking, over the old man's head, but Rutilio didn't react. Except for the slight drumming of his fingers to the rhythm of his tape, he could have been asleep.

'Afternoon,' repeated Justino, getting no more reaction from the old man than before. He pushed the door open and went in.

At a soft touch on the shoulder, Rutilio shot out of his chair, opening his agate eyes. 'What's up?' he asked, removing the earphones.

'It's me, Justino.'

'Hi, long time,' said Rutilio. 'Saddle up anywhere you like.'

Justino sat down next to him. It was the old man's custom to light an oil lamp at nightfall, a polite gesture towards would-be visitors, though few if any ever came any more. His artificial gaze bothered Justino, who otherwise liked him and enjoyed his conversation.

'One of my hens died,' said Rutilio. 'I think it was the heat that done her in.'

There were feathers and droppings in every corner, an acrid odor in the whole place.

'I found out she'd died when the room got full of flies. Trouble is, now the goddam flies won't go away.'

Justino looked up at the fly-spotted ceiling. He was on the point of suggesting DDT, but remembered Rutilio's aversion to pesticides.

'Put up flypaper,' he advised.

The old man smiled. 'No, because I forget where I put it, and then it's me that gets stuck.'

Justino smiled back.

'I won't offer you coffee, because I don't have any,' apologized Rutilio, 'but there's yucca flower boiled with egg in the pot if you want some.'

'No, thanks; I just ate,' answered Justino.

One by one, the hens settled into the nests the old man had made for them under his bed. The cooing of the hens as they tucked their heads under their wings soothed the atmosphere.

The old man showed no sign of knowing about the crime, and Justino didn't know how to ask him about the Gypsy.

Rutilio sensed anxiety in the delegate and turned towards him, his glass eyes flashing in the lamplight.

Justino shuddered. 'They're going to share out more land to the newcomers,' he remarked nervously, trying to cover his confusion.

'How're they going to do that? There are more of them than there are parcels of land,' pointed out Rutilio, waiting, from the silent Justino, for an answer that didn't come.

'What's on your mind?' asked Rutilio straight out.

'I came to ask you something,' said Justino, avoiding the glass eyes.

Rutilio pushed back in his chair. 'Whatever you want, just don't beat around the bush.'

Justino felt like grilling all the Gypsy's mystery out of him: what the Gypsy had been up to that Sunday morning, if he was involved with Adela, the reason for his long stays in Loma Grande, why he had left the village in such a hurry, all of which boiled down to a single question: 'Do you know his shoe size?'

Rutilio cackled, 'He's my friend not my boyfriend,' and laughed again. 'I don't know,' he added, 'but he leaves a bag of clothes here so he doesn't have to drag it around . . . Maybe there's a pair of shoes in it.'

With the ambiguity of his sightlessness, Rutilio waved a hand toward a corner of the room. 'Look over there,' he said.

Justino found a canvas bag, and sat down on the bed to search through it.

'What do you want to know for?' asked Rutilio.

Justino didn't answer; he was holding a pair of sneakers in his hands. The puzzle over the Gypsy's guilt or innocence was solved: the sneakers measured two hand spans. 'Eleven-and-a-half,' exclaimed Justino.

Rutilio turned his head toward him. 'What's José up to?'

he asked, the 'José' emphasizing the familiarity of his relationship with the Gypsy.

Justino heaved a sigh before he answered. 'He's up to his ears,' he said, putting the shoes back in the bag.

'Dames,' said the blind man.

'Yeah, dames,' answered Justino, wanting to add 'and lies': why the hell had Old Friendly invented the scene of struggle and violence between Adela and the Gypsy? What was in it for him? Could he be the real killer? He recalled the absence of bicycle tire marks near the crime scene. Why had Ranulfo sworn he'd been there? Was it to hide something, or just a dumb lie?

Justino stood up to go. He had proved the Gypsy's innocence. But he would do nothing to defend him; he wasn't about to stick his neck out for an outsider he hardly knew.

'It's his ass, not mine,' he thought.

But just to relieve some of the guilt he felt, from the door he said to Rutilio: 'If you see the Gypsy, warn him to be careful; they're out to kill him.'

Rutilio wanted to ask who, but he no longer felt the other's presence in the room.

5

Rutilio was alone again with his hens and his shadows. He put on his earphones, but didn't press the 'play' button. Worried, he was in no mood to listen to music. He was fond of the Gypsy, the only person, his kids included, who cared for him, who gave heed to his blind crabbing and his aged hopelessness. The only one who could stand his shadow-bound clumsiness. Now they were waiting for him to do him in. Rutilio knew perfectly well why: Gabriela Bautista. How many times had he cautioned him not to get tangled up in her skirts. 'You'll come off badly, her husband is a first-class son of a bitch, no holds barred, and if he ever catches you at it, he'll cut you both down.'

The Gypsy would grin defiantly; his scars proved that deceived husbands could do little against him.

'Yes, but Gabriela's husband is of a different stripe,' insisted Rutilio. 'When you least expect it, he'll cut out your guts.'

The Gypsy thanked him for the advice with a clap on the shoulder. 'Don't worry about me, good friend; a bad penny always turns up.'

No doubt the Gypsy had been surprised in his affair with Gabriela Bautista: both were taking greater and greater risks in their encounters. At first they had taken care to appear distant in public; found faraway places and safe nights. Lately they had abandoned all caution and met openly. They sneaked kisses in the street, and fondled each other in the morning in places close to the village. On weekends, when Pedro disappeared from Loma Grande to go and get drunk, Rutilio even had to slip discreetly out of his house so that they could use his bed. Finally, tired of waiting hours for the lovers to finish their thrashing around, and fearful he might be accused of complicity in their adultery and be hurt into the bargain, Rutilio asked them to take their fooling around some-where else. Gabriela and the Gypsy made no protest, figuring the old man was doing enough just by keeping their secret.

At last Pedro Salgado's bloody vengeance, so often pre-dicted by Rutilio, was on the horizon. It seemed inevitable that it should be this way; the Gypsy had risked too much, betting on a married woman. Pedro was in the right as a cheated husband, and could not be reproached for trying to ambush his rival: it was his right to kill him. Rutilio knew he could do nothing to defend his friend, only warn him, put him on the alert. But how, blind as he was? How to spread the word when he could barely move about inside his own four walls? Where to reach him? Whom to trust to find and notify him. He had no choice but to hope that the Gypsy, with his feline instinct, would elude death once more.

6

Justino Téllez swallowed his fury and spat it out wrapped in bile. Old Friendly had taken them all for a ride, and the swindle had taken off at such speed that it was no longer possible to stop it. To the whole village, the fact that the Gypsy had murdered Adela was already an airtight judgment, beyond any proof of innocence. There was no other way but to accept it. Even so, Justino wanted to check one last detail.

He knocked on the door. A half-naked, dirty, sweaty kid opened it.

'Your pa home?' asked Justino.

The kid spun around and Ranulfo Quirarte, Old Friendly, appeared seconds later.

'Afternoon,' he said.

Justino's mouth still tasted of bile, and he would have liked to spit it into the man's face.

'Afternoon,' he responded.

'Come in,' suggested Ranulfo.

'No, thanks; no time.'

Ranulfo squashed a mosquito on his forehead. 'What can I do for you?'

Justino pondered his reply. He had no wish for Old Friendly to realize he had been caught out in his lie.

'Look, Ranulfo, you say you saw the Gypsy last night with the deceased.'

Ranulfo swallowed hard. 'Yeah, well, didn't I tell you already how it happened?'

Justino jerked his chin up as if to say, 'Oh yeah, I remember,' and Ranulfo answered with the same movement, meaning: 'See, you do remember.'

'What was the girl wearing?' asked Justino.

Ranulfo froze, never expecting to be asked that question. He had to improvise.

'It was dark; I couldn't see very well.'

Justino paused.

'Didn't you notice if her blouse was torn?'

Ranulfo's answer was again slow; he could not afford hesitation or contradictions.

'Yes, it was ripped in the struggle.'

'You don't say,' muttered Justino.

'Why all the questions?' inquired Old Friendly.

The delegate wagged his head. 'For the hell of it.'

Ranulfo jerked a thumb inside his house. 'Sure you won't come in? My old woman's cooking some jerked venison.'

Justino smelled the sizzling meat and his mouth watered.

'No, thanks,' he answered, adding, 'but I'll take some if you're offering.'

'Sure thing,' said Ranulfo, turning into the house.

Justino pretended to tie his shoelaces. Squatting, he measured Ranulfo's footstep. He wasn't the murderer either: one span and a finger.

'Shit, the guy's got the foot of a child,' he thought; 'he can't wear more than a size six.'

Old Friendly came back with the salt meat in a plastic bag, and handed it to the delegate.

'Thanks,' said Justino, hefting the bag. 'It's almost a kilo.'

Ranulfo stood in the doorway, waiting for his visitor to say goodbye.

'So long,' muttered Justino, and was on his way when he heard behind him: 'I swear it was them.'

Justino turned around. Old Friendly hadn't budged.

'So help me, I saw them,' said Ranulfo with such conviction that for a moment Justino forgot where the truth really lay.

'I believe you,' he declared, and departed, trying to imagine what Old Friendly had truly seen in the early hours of Sunday morning.

CHAPTER XII

Tuesday

1

Tuesday dawned in the tedious heat of a morning as insipid as any other. The widow Castaños awoke early to the irate squeals of her piglets scraping their snouts against the chicken-wire pen, demanding food. Depressed by her son's tragedy, she had forgotten to feed them for two days. She walked out with the week's bag of leftovers and heaved them over the fence. The pigs started a boisterous battle for the slops, finished them immediately and took up their former station, snouts pressed against the fence. Lacking dried bread and potato peelings, she poured out a roll of sweet cookies for them.

'That's all there is,' she told them as she shook her hands clean.

She did not like to let them run free. Everyone else in the village was in the habit of doing that so they would feed themselves. She was repelled by the possibility that her piglets might eat carrion or excrement. Her cousin Dolores had suffered intestinal aches from eating pork chops infested with bladder-worm.

The sun had not even risen and the day already smelled like a scorcher. The widow went in to cook some beans and sat down to peel garlic. She thought of Gelasio, her elder son, whom she had not seen for more than a year. He had got his green card and was living in Kansas, working as a tractor-driver. It would be Gelasio who could best advise Ramón to control himself and not attack the Gypsy, make it clear to him that it might be he, Ramón, who died in the struggle. But Gelasio was three thousand kilometers away and she, for all her wishes, would have a hard time reining in her youngest son.

The beans began to boil and the widow poured the chopped garlic into the pot. The steam made her perspire even more, so she took a wet cloth to wipe her face. Stepping away from the stove, she walked towards the wall dividing her room from Ramón's. She pulled back the curtain to look at her sleeping son. Though she was terrified by what might happen, she was proud that Ramón had responded like a man. At least he would not be hostage to her fears, nor suffer from behaving like a coward. The widow knew of such disappointments. Graciano Castaños, her dead husband, had carried with him the memory of a youthful cowardice all his life. The memory was so painful that he had never told anyone what happened. All he would say was that he would exchange ten years of his life to return to that fleeting instant in which his lack of decision had made him a coward. Though only he knew what had happened, he had died overcome by that hesitation of long ago.

The widow returned to the stove and put out the fire. She was sick of the steam boiling into the room. It was enough to suffer the overpowering heat of the summer. She felt alone and sad without her husband, with five of her six sons scattered in the world and the sixth trapped in a mortal challenge. Worse still, her best friend, Raquel Rivera, had gone to live in Aguascalientes.

She wished she could wake Ramón, sit him down by her side and satisfy her uncontrollable need to talk for hours, ventilate her monotony, air her hot and humid existence.

She leaned on the window sill, watching the stake truck go by picking up field hands for the Rancho Del Salado cotton fields.

'Six-thirty,' she thought.

She took her coin purse, wiped her sweaty face again and silently left the house to buy milk from Prudencio Negrete.

2

Ramón awoke, chewed up by a night full of visions. Time and time again, he felt Adela breathing beside him. Frightened, he would open his eyes in the darkness and clearly see her hair combed back, her bare forehead, her light eyes and her long naked body. Adela was smiling. Whispering a caress. They were embracing. Ramón felt her soft skin, her gentle breasts, her sensitive belly, her arched torso bathed in blood, the oozing, viscous wound. Terrified, he lurched to the end of the bed, unable to fall asleep until he was sure that Adela's specter had faded from the sheets.

He sat up and heard the truckload of field hands in the distance, on its way to El Salado.

'It's close to seven,' he murmured irritably; he was late. He usually opened the shop at five in the morning. At that hour, even in the half-dark, field hands came to buy soft drinks, potato chips and donuts, and chat for a while before going to work. There was nothing to do in the shop after that until eight in the morning, when women appeared to do their day's shopping.

He sat up on the edge of the mattress. Though worn out

by so many nightmares, he discovered something that bound him even more to Adela: the intense nostalgia for the moments they had not shared. He stood up and looked at himself in the mirror, still wearing the shirt Pedro had lent him. He would have to return it as soon as possible; otherwise his cousin would think he had decided to keep it. Most probably, Pedro was with the rest of the cotton-pickers on their way to El Salado. No matter; he could return the shirt to Gabriela.

He felt worn out, as if he had been cutting cane for three days without rest. His muscles burned and his legs ached. He changed the borrowed shirt for a blue, short-sleeved shirt with a hole in the side. In the kitchen, he added three teaspoons of salt to a glass of water, rinsed his mouth and spat the water onto the dirt floor. An itinerant dentist had recommended this as a daily routine and the best way to get rid of breath that smelled like a dead rat. A glance into his mother's room revealed she was out, so he decided to return the shirt quickly and come back to the shop.

3

He knocked on the door three times, but there was no answer. At the fourth, Gabriela Bautista appeared with the marks of the sheets on her cheeks.

'Hi,' Ramón greeted her.

Gabriela was surprised to see him. It was Ramón who had taken on the commitment to kill the man she loved and she could not understand what he was doing at her house so early.

'What's the matter?' she asked unsociably, on the defensive.

Ramón held the shirt out to her. 'Pedro lent it to me on Sunday and I've come to return it.'

Puzzled, Gabriela accepted the shirt. Somehow, Ramón was her enemy and she wanted to weigh his real intentions.

'Pedro isn't here,' she said flatly.

'I know.'

'Then, what do you want? I'm busy.'

To Ramón, Gabriela's ill humor seemed unusual. She was not habitually rude or bitter.

'Nothing, I don't want anything,' answered Ramón, thinking that Gabriela's aggressiveness was due to just getting up. Wasting no more time upsetting her, he said, 'Say hello to my cousin for me,' and he walked away quickly.

'Jesus Christ!' grumbled Gabriela furiously and slammed the door. She was angry and irritated. Ramón's visit had her spinning. She took a deep breath to get hold of herself, but was unable to get rid of the twister inside her. Desire, love, passion, pleasure, guilt – all fused into one overwhelming sense of horror. Horror of the absurd circumstances, of a stupid, sinister vengeance, put together out of a misunderstanding. Horror of her role as clandestine lover, of her reiterated condition of wife. Horror of the Gypsy, of Pedro, of Ramón. Horror, above all, of herself. That was what most upset her: her fear of openly saving the life of the man she loved. It was not a matter of saving him from a mere boy whose hands would no doubt tremble as he tried to kill him, but from an entire village, insatiably pursuing the wrong crime. She would have to defend him from the same people who would stone her if she dared tell the truth. She must therefore keep silent. Remain silent to survive, but to survive only by half, gnawed within by her weakness and mediocre indecisiveness.

She emptied a glass of water over her head, something she did every summer morning. It was her grandmother's way of relieving the heat. The water trickled through her tangled hair, cooling her skull and neck. She remembered her grandmother sitting in a rocking chair, her legs a mass of sores, terminally ill and lamenting the many things she had been unable to experience, for which there was no longer any possible remedy.

'I stayed here,' she would say to Gabriela, 'roasting in this foul heat because I never imagined one would really die. Had I known it sooner, I would have got out of here a long time ago. But now I'm a wreck and I can't go anywhere. The worst of it is that I can't find the goddam gearshift to put me in reverse, and send me back.'

Then the old woman would laugh, repeating 'The gearshift, the goddam gearshift,' making fun of her atrophied legs, of her festering pustules, of her life snuffed out in the heat of the sun, of the painful toothmarks of death. The day before her last, the old woman had murmured into her granddaughter's ear: 'I don't want to die.' She was buried the next afternoon.

Gabriela had promised herself she would not repeat her grandmother's mindless existence. She would make of her life what she wished. But it was not to be. Like the old woman, she remained embedded in the dust, helplessly seeking to find the gearshift that would make it possible to turn back the clock. She poured another glass of water over her head and then another, and another, until she was completely soaked. She drew the curtains, undressed, climbed into bed and switched on the radio. She listened to tropical music for a while until she heard a pick-up approaching the village by the road from the reservoir.

'It's him,' she thought. 'It must be him.' In a rush, she put on her dress and ran to the door, intending to jump out and intercept him as soon as he was in sight. She would climb into the cab and run away with him. That way she would save his life and her own at the same time.

She remained tense for a few seconds, her throat dry and her eyes glued to the road. Disappointment came with the knowledge that it was not the Gypsy coming, but two gray-blue pick-ups, at top speed, raising clouds of dust.

4

'The cows are on strike,' said Prudencia Negrete. 'Today they've given hardly any milk.'

Astrid Monge and Anita Novoa forced a smile at the remark. The old Negrete woman was a handful, unstable, known to blow up over nothing. But this morning she was in a good mood. 'Sell me at least five liters,' begged Astrid, whose mother turned it into cheese, which she then sold to the evangelists of the Pastores Ejido.

'I don't have any left; the Nestlé truck took what little there was,' said Prudencia in all honesty. Nestlé's buyer had come very early for the twelve liters produced by the woman's five cows.

Discreetly, Anita pointed out to Astrid a drum oozing milk.

'And what's that?' asked Astrid.

Prudencia turned to look at the drum and smiled. 'It's useless, curdled milk from an infected cow; if you want it, it's yours,' she said, taking a few unsteady steps and extracting a glass jar from the cupboard. 'I've got this half-liter of fresh cream; want it?'

Astrid shook her head but Anita accepted the jar.

'I'll take it,' she said. 'How much?'

Prudencia did some arithmetic on the fingers of her left hand.

'Give me three pesos,' she answered and went on talking to Astrid: 'You know, you can reserve the milk; just pay me beforehand.'

'OK, keep ten liters for me,' said Astrid and handed her a twenty-peso note.

'Let me see if I have any change,' said Prudencia, turning into the house to look for it.

Anita and Astrid heard a 'Good day' and turned to find the widow Castaños coming to buy milk. The woman was obviously worried.

'Where's Prudencia?' she asked.

'She'll be right back,' answered Anita.

The three women fell silent, wishing to avoid the subject hanging over them: the widow because of the anguish it caused her; Astrid, so as not to show how much she knew; and Anita, not wishing to get involved in something that had nothing to do with her.

Prudencia came out with the twenty-peso note still in her hand.

'I don't have any change,' she said, stopping short in front of the widow as if she had seen a ghost.

'Hello,' said the widow.

'What's new, Pancha?' responded Prudencia, not knowing what else to say.

'Have you any milk?'

'No, it's all gone.'

The widow looked down and stood, undecided. It

seemed that the lack of milk had made her particularly sad. Astrid felt a desire to reveal the truth, but she didn't, deciding to leave her in peace.

From where she was standing, Prudencia recognized the rural police crossing the highway at top speed.

'Here come the rangers,' she said. The widow turned and saw the pick-ups park in front of Justino Téllez' house.

5

Justino had barely heard the motors being turned off when he discovered Carmelo Lozano peering at him through the window.

'What's up, beast with claws?' shouted the captain.

Justino leaned back lazily in his breakfast chair. 'Just hanging out, beast with hoofs,' he answered dully, bored with their old formula.

'Aren't you going to offer me some?' asked Carmelo.

Justino spread his arms. 'Do I have a choice?' he answered without looking at him.

The captain lifted a long leg over the window sill and entered the house.

'There's a door for that,' complained Justino.

Carmelo gave him a mocking grin. 'I know, but that's how I remember the steaming nights I visited your sister.'

Since Justino had no sisters, the policeman's crude joke made no impression.

Carmelo pulled up a chair and sat down at the table. 'What are you going to give me for breakfast?'

Justino didn't answer, but uncovered a pot containing three fried mojarras.

'They'll make a good taco,' said Carmelo. 'Pass me a tortilla.'

Justino shoved the tortilla basket toward him. Carmelo carefully stripped one of the fish from its bones, put the flesh in a tortilla, squeezed lemon juice onto it, salted it and put it away in four bites.

With the same care, the captain made himself three more tacos and then asked Justino for two bananas, which he devoured instantly. Finally, he asked if Justino knew when the baseball game would be broadcast from Tampico.

'At eight tonight,' answered Justino, for something to say.

Carmelo listened attentively, repeated 'At eight tonight,' stood up and thanked his friend for the breakfast.

'Don't mention it,' answered Justino, knowing that Carmelo would not be long in bringing up his professional insight.

Wiping the residue of oil and fish from his mouth with a piece of toilet paper, the captain rolled up his sleeves, threw back his head and sighed: 'You and I know, partner,' he said, 'that you know a lot about what happened here on Sunday, understand?'

'I don't understand a damned thing,' answered Justino, annoyed.

Carmelo put his hands to his forehead. 'I'll try again,' he said. Taking his hand from his head he traced an oval in the air and continued, 'Look, partner, I'll make it clear: if I find out there's one more corpse in this village because of that girl that was murdered, you'll be the first I'll go after. One mistake and I'll lock you up.'

Justino well knew Carmelo's style of feigned and provocative threats, but he decided to play along.

'Go after the troublemakers, why me?'

Lozano smiled. 'Because you're fat and old and easy to catch. The others run fast. Furthermore, didn't you say you're the law around here?'

'So?'

'Who besides you is going to be responsible?'

'That's the point,' argued Justino; 'let me handle things here my way. You go back to Ciudad Mante and later I'll let you know how it all turned out.'

Carmelo took Justino by the arm and feinted a hook to the liver. Justino pretended to dodge it.

'You never change, friend; you're just as pig-headed as ever,' said the captain, adding, 'OK, I won't give you a hard time.'

Carmelo opened the door to go out and was met by a wave of hot air in his face. Shading his eyes from the glaring light with the palm of his hand, he said, 'What a scorcher. You could broil a chicken in it.'

Justino walked to the door and raised his eyes to a cloudless sky. Lowering them again, he found Carmelo's eight men roasting in the heat while they waited for their boss. Justino looked at them with a touch of pity.

'It's your boys that are broiling,' he said sarcastically.

'That's why they're here,' said Carmelo indifferently. 'Anyway, they needed some sun.'

He turned to his subordinates and with a finger motioned one of them over. The man jumped out of the truck and stood to attention in front of Carmelo.

'Yes, sir, Captain.'

Carmelo looked the cop up and down.

'Sergeant Garcés, do you like baseball?'

'Yes, sir.'

With a smack of the tongue, Carmelo drew Justino's attention. 'You heard that? He likes baseball.'

Irritated, Justino nodded.

'What's your favorite team, Sergeant?' continued Carmelo.

'The Tampico Stevedores.'

'Are they good?'

'Yes, sir.'

'And what do you do when you can't go to the game?'

'I listen to it on the radio.'

'Great, are they playing today?'

'Yes, sir.'

'At what time?'

'At six in the afternoon.'

'At six, not at eight?'

'No, sir, at six.'

'Are you sure?'

'Yes, sir.'

'Thank you, Sergeant. Dismissed.'

The policeman turned back to his pick-up and Carmelo reproached Justino.

'You're either a liar or live on the moon.'

'Or I don't like baseball,' corrected Justino.

'So, why invent a broadcast at eight?'

Justino shrugged.

'That's why you want me to trust you?' asked the captain sarcastically.

'Just like that.'

Carmelo put an arm over Justino's shoulders and pulled him with him towards the vehicle.

'When it turns cold, we'll go duck-shooting, OK?'

'Sure,' said Justino. They had gone hunting together before, at the expense of the rural police, who provided ammunition and sawed-off shotguns.

Carmelo opened the door, rolled down the window and

climbed into the seat. 'See you, partner,' he said. 'Don't let this turn into a massacre.'

Sergeant Garcés climbed out of the back and got behind the wheel. The other policemen got into either vehicle.

'When you've made up your mind, let me know who killed the girl. Meantime, keep an eye on Ramón, in case he loses his head and wants to take revenge.'

The captain and his men took off. Justino had no doubt that Carmelo Lozano could smell blood at any distance.

CHAPTER XIII

A Double-barreled .25-caliber Davis Derringer

1

On Sunday night, he bought a batch of twenty portable tape recorders he had negotiated with Lorenzo Marquez, the smuggler, and by Monday afternoon he had sold eighteen of them at two hundred pesos apiece, having paid seventy-five. They were bought by a team of reaper-operators who, that very Monday morning, had finished their contract for ninety hectares of sorghum. The Gypsy was lucky enough to find them, half drunk and loaded with money, where the railroad crossed the highway. They were waiting in a nearby truck stop, while repairs were made to the engine that was to haul away their gigantic reapers. It was an easy sale for the Gypsy because, as soon as one of them bought a tape recorder, the rest felt obliged to do the same so as to keep up appearances.

That night, he slept on the flatcars along with the operators. He was awakened by the locomotive jerking the string of flatcars into motion. Dropping quickly to the ground, he watched the train head south toward Abasolo. As day broke, he walked to the truck stop, which had already been open for some time. He ordered coffee with milk and scrambled eggs with dried beef. He had earned two thousand pesos in one day, enough to keep him comfortably for the rest of the month, and decided not to work for at least a week.

The waitress who brought his breakfast was slim and

attractive, with fine features and round buttocks. Had he not been busy, thinking about what he would do for the next few days, he would have made a pass at her. As it was, he paid no attention.

With all that money in hand, his plans changed. He had intended to visit the settlements around Casas, even visit Las Menonas, where more than one modernized Mennonite liked to buy his electronic gadgets and now and then even some fake jewelry. After that, he was going down to Ciudad Mante, stopping to sell in the villages along the highway, so as to return to Loma Grande in two or three weeks. But now he had more than enough time and didn't know what to do, or where to go.

He ordered some sweet buns to dunk in his coffee, but the girl told him there were none, and he had to settle for some Wonder pound cakes. They tasted good but quickly fell apart in the coffee, so he had eventually to spoon them out.

Pushing aside his empty cup, he put his elbows on the table and pondered which way to go. He could continue toward Soto La Marina to spend a few days in the Laguna Madre, or to Cadereyta for a rodeo or a bullfight, or head for Tampico to see relatives and friends, and a whore or two in the brothel of his youth. After considering several options, he decided on Los Aztecas.

This was the most developed of the villages around the Las Animas reservoir. It boasted four hundred inhabitants and electricity, cement-block houses, a telephone booth, three paved streets and a gas station. He had chosen Los Aztecas for two basic reasons: first, it was there that cotton-dealing generated sporadic but substantial operations in which he could invest his money; and, second and decisively, it was only twenty kilometers from Loma Grande.

He asked for the check, paid for his breakfast and bought a cheap paper, published in San Fernando, from a kid outside. The headlines reported a round-up of satanic homosexuals in Nuevo Laredo and the waste and excess of a local official. The Gypsy flipped the four printed pages, crumpled them into a ball and threw it away.

'The same as always,' he thought.

The kid picked up the paper, smoothed the pages and put it back with the rest of his newspapers to be sold again.

2

By ten o'clock in the morning, they were already installed in Ramón's shop. Sitting on metal chairs painted in the colors and logo of Pepsi Cola, Torcuato Garduño, Pascual Ortega and Macedonio Macedo were drinking beer, avid for news of how things were going, for every detail of how Ramón intended to eliminate his enemy. After the usual round of nonsense, Pascual decided to ask Ramón straight out: 'Have you decided how you're going to kill him?'

'No,' answered Ramón.

Torcuato got up from his chair and stood next to him. 'Well, think about it,' he said, 'because you're not going to get the Gypsy just like that.'

It would be a few weeks before the Gypsy came back to Loma Grande, if he came back at all. It was his habit to show up in the village on the first Friday of each month. There was plenty of time to plan the killing, as Macedonio pointed out.

'What if he shows up right now?' asked Torcuato. 'Are we going to let him find out and get away alive and well? No sir, this has to be decided right now. Ramón has to be ready for whenever the son of a bitch comes back.'

They agreed and, among the four of them, planned countless ways to carry out the murder, discarding them one after the other. To bushwhack him in the gullies was difficult, not only because the Gypsy was always on the look-out, but because to carry it out they would need a shotgun, and only two people in Loma Grande owned one: Omar Carrillo, who had a flintlock which sometimes fired and sometimes didn't, a risky weapon for this kind of business; and Ranulfo Quirarte – Old Friendly – who wouldn't lend anyone his 16-gauge single shot. To attack the man with a machete was no good either: since they had carved up his back, the Gypsy never let anyone armed with a machete get within three meters of him.

After discarding a number of alternatives, the four decided the best way for Ramón to kill him was with a pistol, a small weapon that could be easily handled. However, there was one matter that would have to be solved: the army had recently carried out a surprise and very effective campaign against handguns throughout the area. Only a lucky few had been able to hide theirs and escape confiscation. Among the latter, the only one who was trustworthy was Juan Prieto, Ramón's best friend. All that remained was to find out if he had ammunition and, most important, if he would lend the weapon.

Juan Prieto was the same age as Ramón but looked older. At fifteen, he had emigrated as a wetback and been lucky enough to get as far as Portland, Oregon, where the arrest of illegals by immigration agents was almost unknown. He had got a job washing dishes in a Chinese restaurant. After four months, he switched to cleaning bathrooms for an insurance company and from there went back to dishwashing at a dive called Suzie's Bar, run by an immense woman who changed the color of her hair every week. Juan Prieto had lasted there only three months, because Susan Blackwell, the fat lady, turned him in to immigration so as not to have to pay him his back wages.

Juan remembered his arrest as a nightmare: four men, three in civilian clothes, and one in an unrecognizable uniform, came into the bar and jumped him as soon as they saw him. Juan immediately realized what was happening and tried to flee between the tables. A customer stuck out his foot and Juan fell on his face. The man in the uniform clubbed him on the floor. Juan tried to protect his head with his arms, but couldn't prevent a blow to his head, a cracked rib and a splintered elbow.

He was cuffed, his feet tied, gagged and thrown into the trunk of a car. In that condition, he was taken on a ride that lasted hours to a village he did not recognize. There, he was taken out and handed over to men in other uniforms. They put him into a van, still cuffed, but minus the gag and the ropes on his feet and took him to a building in San Francisco. In a glass-walled office, a translator informed him that he was under arrest for illegal residence in the country, resisting arrest, striking an officer and robbery. He was further informed that the district attorney would withdraw the charges if he signed papers undertaking never to return to the United States. Juan signed. They fingerprinted, photographed and booked him, and five days later, deported him to Tijuana in another van.

In Tijuana, other wetbacks explained that his lightning deportation was typical of denunciations by crooked employers. Accusations of robbery were frequent in such cases. Infuriated by the trick, Juan found a way to return to Portland and get even with the fat lady, and by the way collect his belongings from the rooming house where he had lived.

He had crossed the border again, hidden in a loaded trailer. In San Diego, he picked up some money by rolling a Portuguese sailor he found lying blind-drunk on a sidewalk. It paid for a Greyhound ticket to Sacramento; but it took him two months more to get to Portland.

There, he picked up his belongings, including eight hundred dollars he had saved, sewing them into the seams of a pair of trousers. The manager was an old black alcoholic, whose memories of past glory had to do with the time he played bass in B. B. King's first band.

The afternoon of his arrival, Juan carefully cased Susan Blackwell's bar. It was her habit to leave the place at four in the morning, after closing up and clearing accounts. That morning she made no change in her routine. As she was getting into her car, Juan clubbed her on the head, and then again and again.

She fell to the pavement, her green hair soaked in blood. Thinking she was dead, Juan grabbed her bag and ran through the still city streets.

He returned to Mexico full of fear, regretting his violent behavior. On his way, he bought a pocket pistol offered to him in a bus terminal. It was a double-barreled .25 caliber

Davis Derringer, which cost him fifty dollars. He taped it into the lining of his hat, ready for use on the first cop who tried to arrest him. There was no need. He reached the border at Eagle Pass, opposite Piedras Negras, changing buses from time to time, and there crossed the river on an inflated tractor inner-tube.

He had returned to Loma Grande a year after his departure, but refrained from living in the village owing to his unrelenting fear that someday an American squad car would pick him up. He built himself a hut on a bank of the reservoir, where he watched over Lucio and Pedro Estrada's fishing gear and boats.

4

The Gypsy parked his pick-up beside the gas pump and handed over the key.

'Make it forty pesos worth of Nova.' He got out and walked to the shop beside the gas station to buy a can of beer and, settling on the cooler, drank it. He was tired. The drive to Los Aztecas in the midday heat, on a highway crowded with trailers, had worn him out. He drank the beer, taking pleasure in the foam bubbling down his throat. When the attendant gestured that he had finished gassing up, the Gypsy finished his beer, paid and climbed in.

He felt like a shower and a nap. He knew of a rooming house, the Albatross, where he stayed on and off, and where, for thirty-five pesos, he could have a room with a large bed, private bath, standing fan, breakfast and supper included. The owner, known as La Chata Fernández, managed the establishment with the help of her adolescent daughter Margarita; both were attentive and cheerful. The Gypsy liked to stay there, not only for the service but because both women were great talkers, full of the latest information for clients staying overnight. It occurred to him they might inform him of anything unusual happening in Loma Grande, whether the man who had shone a light on them that early Sunday morning had identified them and if anything had come of it.

The rooming house was located in an old, one-story building with six rooms around a central living room. Dining room and kitchen were separate from them in another structure. La Chata Fernández had designed it that way with her former partner, Silvia Espinoza, who had left the business when she married a Spanish traveling salesman. Thanks to his friendship with La Chata, the Gypsy could pick the bedroom of his choice, the one in the middle facing north and therefore the coolest.

In spite of the suffocating afternoon, he showered with water as hot as possible.

'Heat overcomes heat,' he thought.

He came out of the bathroom with a towel around his waist, opened a window and closed the mosquito netting. A roach appeared beneath the curtain, trying to hide under the chest of drawers. He squashed it with his bare foot, hearing it crunch underneath, and sat down on the bed to wipe his sole. Removing the towel, he spread it on the pillow so as not to soak it with his wet hair. Then he lay down and fell sleep.

When he awoke, it was seven-fifteen. Supper was always served at seven-thirty sharp. He dressed quickly, knowing from Margarita that the menu included prawn soup, Mexican rice and tongue in tomato sauce, and he didn't want to miss it.

By the time he entered the dining room, most of the other guests were already seated. Some of them he knew: Carlos Gutiérrez, a hydraulic engineer who supervised the area's irrigation systems; Felipe Fierro, a civil engineer who directed paving operations on the highway from Abra to Los Aztecas; and Javier Belmont, a dentist who had retired to the cotton business. The others, an elderly couple and a short, tired-eyed woman, he had never seen.

After supper, only Margarita, La Chata, Felipe Fierro and the Gypsy remained to chat. Anxious for news, the Gypsy asked La Chata a few questions. Corrected now and then by her daughter washing dishes in the kitchen, she put her elbows on the table and supplied the most important news: another marihuana plantation discovered in Nuevo Morelos; rice fields belonging to the oilworker's union sold to a federal legislator; ten thousand pesos won on a Pepsi Cola bottle-cap promotion by a member of the Plan de Ayala Ejido; tourists held up at González; a letter sent by a campesino from the Niños Héroes Ejido answered by the governor, and cattle at Rancho la Paloma infested with screw worm. As she mentioned nothing of interest to him, the Gypsy asked, 'What do you hear from Loma Grande?'

La Chata thought for a moment, pursed her lips and shook her head. 'Nothing I can think of.'

Margarita came out of the kitchen drying a plate and, leaning against the door jamb, added, measuring her words: 'I heard that a girl was killed there on Sunday.'

The Gypsy felt as if his lungs had been pierced. He controlled his nerves and slowly inquired, 'Where did you hear that?'

'Dulcineo Sosa told me this morning, when I went to the market for prawns.'

'Did he tell you her name?' he asked, hoping Margarita would mention another.

'Yes, but I've already forgotten it.'

The Gypsy swallowed: 'Gabriela?'

The girl thought for a moment and answered in the affirmative: 'That's it,' she said. 'That was the name he told me.'

Seeing the Gypsy pale, La Chata asked him: 'Did you know her?'

The Gypsy barely nodded. 'Just by sight. Her husband used to buy things from me,' he answered as a drop of sweat slid from his neck down his back.

5

Juan Prieto tensed when he heard voices from the turn in the road. The presence of strangers near the ramp made him nervous, invariably reminding him of American cops coming to arrest him. Then he recognized the voices of Ramón and Torcuato, and came out from behind the tree where he was hiding.

'What's up?' he greeted them.

Ramón and the rest responded in a gabble of unrelated words. Frightened by the noise, a coot took off through the rushes at the edge of the reservoir, leaving an arrow-shaped wake in the still water. Sunlight glinted on fish scales lying around the boats.

Juan pointed to a long net. 'Give me a hand to spread it out.'

They tied the hundred-meter net to a number of posts. It revealed countless holes and tears, which Juan was required to repair with jute twine. It would take him all morning.

After spreading the net, they retired to some rocks. One of them held an up-turned turtle shell, with the remains of flesh still in it. Macedonio Macedo aimed a kick at it so that he could sit on the rock, but Juan stopped him.

'Leave it alone, I'm drying it out for the shell.'

Macedonio protested: 'It stinks.'

Torcuato picked it up and examined it. 'It's useless,' he said; 'it's cracked.'

'Then throw it away,' said Juan.

'Next time put in salt or ash,' suggested Pascual, 'then it won't stink and get full of worms.'

'Or scrape it out,' added Torcuato.

The five of them sat down on the rocks, while Juan remarked on last month's large tilapia catch.

Macedonio asked if there were any they could cook for lunch.

'No,' answered Juan, 'but I can net some right now.'

Standing up, he took off his T-shirt and asked Ramón to go with him.

'We'll make a fire in the meantime,' said Torcuato.

Juan and Ramón walked to the edge of the reservoir, removed their shoes and rolled up their pants clear of the water. Juan picked up the cast net and Ramón a tin bucket. Together they waded into the water, startling a dozen frogs, which jumped out of their way in the mud.

Juan swung the net, let the lead weights sink and pulled it in. There were no fish.

'No luck,' he said, swinging the net again. At the same time, a pelican dived into the water a few meters away.

'That's where the mojarra are; let's go further out,' he proposed. They advanced until the water was up to their knees. 'We'll surely get some here.'

They fell silent as Juan swung the net again without success.

'We'll have to go in deeper,' suggested Ramón. They kept on another twenty paces until they were wet to their waists. Juan swung the net and, as he pulled it in, felt its weight.

'Now I got some,' he said, raising the net. Three tilapia were flapping desperately in its folds.

'I heard about your girlfriend,' murmured Juan, as he hooked the gills of a mojarra to pull it out of the net; 'that was really awful.'

Ramón was ashamed to keep up the lie of his fake romance before his friend. He ought to confess that his relationship with Adela had barely begun the day they killed her. But he didn't: he couldn't betray a woman who had left him a coded expression of love in obscure letters – much less betray the love he himself felt for a nude, warm body in his arms, for a girl photographed in three-quarter profile in black and white, for an absence that was spreading inside him. To reveal the truth to Juan meant the chance of freeing himself from the overwhelming commitment to kill another: his last way out. He decided to cut it off.

'Yeah, it was awful,' he added.

Juan pulled a fish out of the net and threw it into Ramón's bucket.

'Pedro told me you're going to get even.'

'That's why I need the loan of your pistol.'

Juan freed another fish and dropped it into the bucket. Were it anyone else, he would not lend the weapon; especially as he knew beyond a doubt that it would be used to kill someone. But Ramón being his childhood friend, he could not refuse.

'Sure. As soon as we finish here, I'll give it to you,' he said without turning to look at Ramón.

They caught six more mojarras, left the reservoir and found Torcuato squatting before some wet wood he was trying to ignite. Beside him, Macedonio was blowing on the sparks, trying to get a flame going. Juan handed the fish to Pascual for cleaning while he and Ramón went to the hut for the pistol.

Inside, Juan dug into a sack of dry corn until he felt the Derringer. He cleaned it by blowing off the dust and husks, then crossed the room to take down four cartridges hidden on a beam.

'They're all I've got,' he said. He broke the pistol, slipped the cartridges into the chambers and, snapping it shut, handed it to Ramón.

'It's ready,' he said, pointing to the trigger. 'There's no safety; you just cock the hammer.'

To Ramón, the weapon in the palm of his hand was like a toy, the little bullets in their shiny brass casing, as well.

'Can you really kill someone with this little piece of junk?'

'If you hit the right place, yes . . . If not, no.'

Ramón cocked the pistol and pointed at random.

'Watch it,' barked Juan; 'don't let off a shot by mistake.'

Ramón unloaded the pistol and, holding it in his hand, aimed it at Juan. He held the sight on his chest and pulled the trigger.

'It's not so easy,' remarked Juan at the sound of the click.

'What isn't?'

'To blow someone away.'

Ramón shrugged his shoulders.

'The worst of it,' continued Juan, 'is that afterwards

there's no way you can get the victim out of your head,'
and he sighed, still overcome by the memory of the obese
American woman, covered with blood after he had beaten
her.

Without a word, Ramón lowered the pistol he had been
holding at the ready.

'Do you know what you're getting into?' asked Juan.

'No,' answered Ramón simply, putting the Derringer
and its .25 caliber bullets in his right pants pocket.

6

The Gypsy awoke, bathed in perspiration, drowning in
recurrent dreams of Gabriela cut to pieces, Gabriela
devoured by worms, Gabriela far away, Gabriela dead,
Gabriela lost for ever. He kicked off the sheets and turned
on the lamp on the bedside table. Rubbing his eyes, dazzled by the dim yellowish light, he looked out the window
into the moonless night. On the other side of the mosquito
netting, he could hear the sharp cries of bats hunting
insects.

He wanted to smoke, and put his bag on the bed to
search for a pack of cigarettes. He kept rummaging, fully
aware that he would find nothing, for he had quit smoking
ten months before. He closed the bag, put on his pants and
a shirt, pulled back the wire mosquito net and jumped into
the garden. He could feel the sharp grass against the soles
of his bare feet. In the darkness, he distinguished a tiled
path that went around the bedrooms towards the street.
He followed it until he reached the fence. A toad jumped
beside him. He pushed it away with his heel and it
continued on its way among the potted plants.

Careful to make no noise, he drew the bolt on the gate. Stepping out, he began to walk towards the illuminated part of the village in the hope of finding someone who would give him a cigarette. He reached the light but found no one, then turned to the plaza and found it deserted. He sat down on a bench to watch the moths fluttering around the street lamps. The mayor had told him that soon all the villages in the region would have electric light. The Gypsy didn't believe it: he didn't believe politicians or women.

He didn't even believe Gabriela Bautista when she told him she loved him and she was willing to leave everything for him. He hadn't believed it until that very moment.

He began to walk around the plaza, irritated by the hum of the generator breaking the silence of the night. He wanted the silence, to think, and evoke Gabriela. He remembered the morning in August when they had been making love in the back of his pick-up parked at the edge of a muddy dirt road. He recalled the gray horizon over the green crops, rain pattering on the canvas cover. He remembered the look in her deep eyes, her shiny skin, her legs around him, the dampness of her. He remembered their last night together, the chase by lamplight, the race into the underbrush, their intimacy torn apart, their secret discovered, their last love. He imagined Gabriela dead and felt like setting fire to Loma Grande before doing the same to himself.

He returned when flocks of white heron were beginning their morning flight over the rice paddies. As dawn was breaking, he climbed through the window into his room. He stripped, feeling the heat more unbearable than ever at that hour. Finally he fell on the bed and lay there on his back, his eyes fixed on the fan turning beside him.

*

He did not emerge from the room until late, having bathed and dressed lazily, caught up in a strange fatigue. Only the elderly couple he did not know were in the dining room. He greeted them and remained standing without knowing in which of the nine chairs to sit. La Chata came out of the kitchen carrying a steaming casserole, which she deposited on the table.

'Hi.'

'Hi.'

'Did you oversleep?'

'Yeah.'

'Will you have beans?'

'Yes,' answered the Gypsy and sat down slowly in the chair in front of him.

La Chata served him, aware that she had never seen the Gypsy so depressed.

The old couple finished their breakfast and retired. The Gypsy began to eat his plate of beans slowly.

'Stop suffering,' said La Chata, smiling.

The Gypsy turned to look at her, disconcerted by her attitude, which seemed to be making fun of him.

'Suffering from what?' he asked aggressively.

La Chata smiled again, made a pellet out of a piece of bread and threw it to a white cat playing with a dead grasshopper by the kitchen door.

'It wasn't the one you thought that was killed.' She continued watching the cat eat the bread, and added, 'Margarita got the name wrong.'

La Chata's revelation confused the Gypsy; he was not sure she was serious.

'The girl that was stabbed to death in Loma Grande was called Adela, not Gabriela.'

'How do you know?'

'The evangelists told me. She was one of the new-comers. They buried her Sunday evening.'

'What else?'

'Nothing. The evangelists haven't been back to Loma Grande since then and don't know what else may have happened.'

The Gypsy shivered with relief and La Chata pulled her chair closer until she was only a few centimeters away from him.

'Listen up,' she said; 'leave that Gabriela alone unless you really want her killed.'

'What are you talking about?'

La Chata leaned back. 'About how you love to play the fool. What made you think the dead girl might have been called Gabriela?'

The Gypsy smiled.

'It's obvious that Gabriela has you running in circles. Remember the saying: a married woman – either you touch her in passing, or you steal her away . . .'

The Gypsy finished his breakfast and stood up.

'Thanks,' he said.

'What for?' asked La Chata.

'For the beans, they were very good . . .'

Lying on the bed, the Gypsy ruminated: all those nerves and anguish because he believed Gabriela dead could mean only one thing: he was in love with her and ought to take her away. There was no way out; he would go back to Loma Grande next day to get her.

He closed his eyes and tried to make up for the hours of sleep he'd lost the night before.

CHAPTER XIV

The Best Way to Kill Him

1

He walked five paces from the nopal, cocked the pistol and raised his arm in that direction. Squeezing his left eye shut, he tried to fix the target in the sight. Though he held his breath to steady his aim, he could not stop the Derringer weaving from side to side. Clutching the butt tightly, he fired as soon as he felt sure of his aim, then, with both eyes open, examined the nopal.

Torcuato shook his head in disapproval. 'You missed,' he declared, arms crossed.

Juan Prieto examined the nopal carefully for a hole anywhere in it, but there was none. The shot had come nowhere close. Ramón relaxed his grip and lowered the pistol.

'You aimed too high,' said Pascual. 'I saw a puff of dust on the hill.'

It turned out not to be as simple to hit the target as Ramón had thought. The Derringer was too small and too light; he couldn't get a good grip on it. It was almost impossible to keep the barrel steady.

'You're going to have to put the pistol close to his head,' said Macedonio; 'you can't shoot worth a damn.'

Torcuato reacted: 'Yeah, and the Gypsy's going to let Ramón get that close? No sir, he's got to learn to hit the target at a distance.' He took the pistol from Ramón, broke it, removed the empty shell, blew out the remains of burnt powder in the chamber, moistened his palm with saliva and cocked the pistol again.

'Watch,' he said to Ramón; 'the trick is not to lock your elbow.'

Torcuato stood with his legs apart parallel to the target. He raised his arm, elbow bent at a right angle, took a deep breath, aimed and slowly squeezed the trigger. The shot echoed off the side of the dam. Torcuato raised his head to get a better look at the trajectory of the bullet.

'Nothing,' said Juan. 'You fired even higher than Ramón.'

Torcuato challenged him with a raised chin.

'Bigmouth, you're blind.' He walked to the nopal and examined it on all sides in search of his shot, finally admitting that he had missed, with a categorical 'The sight's crooked on this stupid little toy.'

Crooked or not, it seemed evident to Ramón that it would be hard to kill the Gypsy with the Derringer. He would have to shoot at very close range, preferably at the temple or between the eyes. 'The way you shoot javelina when they charge you,' he said to Macedonio.

Nor did Ramón himself know if he would have the nerve, when the time came, to go up to the Gypsy and shoot him point-blank.

By three o'clock in the afternoon, most of the inhabitants of Loma Grande knew that Ramón Castaños was planning to kill his rival with a pistol borrowed from Juan Prieto. 'The same one he used to blast a policeman in Texas,' said those who did not know Juan's real story. The word also got around that it was a tricky pistol that didn't shoot straight. The question brought a number of men to the store to discuss the advantages or disadvantages of using the Derringer. Opinions flew back and forth.

'I think that tiny pistol is just the thing,' said Ethiel Cervera. 'The Gypsy will never know what Ramón has in his hand.'

'But the bullets are just as tiny,' interrupted Amador; 'if Ramón doesn't shoot him square in the head, the Gypsy's going to get him.'

'Yeah, they look like rabbit shot,' said Lucio.

'Hell no, I've killed deer with smaller ones than that, with a .22; I could even get a wildcat with a .22,' said Sirenio, the youngest Pérez, with conviction.

'Bullshit,' jibed Lucio. 'When have you ever shot a goddam deer?'

Sirenio was going to continue the argument, but Torcuato intervened. 'What you've got to do,' he said to Ramón, 'is kill him without letting him see you.'

'In the back?' injected Macedonio. 'That's no way for a man.'

'It was real macho of the Gypsy to stab the girl in the back, wasn't it?' objected Torcuato.

'You're right there,' admitted Macedonio and continued advising Ramón: 'Well, yes, then shoot him in the back.'

'And how is he going to do that if the goddam Gypsy always walks close to the wall?' asked Amador.

'That's true, the son of a bitch is always on the look-out,' added Pedro Estrada.

They were still deep in their discussion when Marcelino arrived. Had anyone noticed the look in his eye, they would have realized he was looking for trouble.

'Forget all the jabber,' he interrupted; 'the Gypsy would be a damn fool to come back here.'

The others fell silent. Nobody had considered the possibility of an inconclusive revenge. They all took it for granted that the Gypsy would come back to Loma Grande at the beginning of the following month.

'He wouldn't be that dumb,' continued Marcelino, 'or do you think he is going to bring her flowers?'

Without moving from the chair, or putting down his beer, Justino Téllez declared: 'He'll be back, you can bet on it.'

Marcelino turned on him with a crooked smile.

'Who are you to talk? You've already spilled to Carmelo Lozano. You think we don't know he went to your house this morning?'

Justino took a pull at his bottle, put his hands behind his head and, without a sign of irritation, answered, 'Spilled? Your mother, ass-hole. If you don't know what I told Carmelo, keep your mouth shut.'

The widow Castaños, who heard everything from the other side of the wall, went into the shop expecting trouble. She crossed the circle of men, murmuring a 'Good afternoon' to all, asked Lucio Estrada after the health of Evelia, Pedro Estrada about Rosa's condition, and sat down on a stool next to the counter.

Her maneuver was successful: the tension dissipated. Conversation began again on a variety of different matters, until little by little the Derringer took over again.

The argument continued for a long while with no sign of reaching a conclusion. At five in the afternoon the group had become considerably larger. The new arrivals quickly joined one side or the other, arguing the pros and cons of the Derringer. The debate wandered into absurd considerations about the correlation between the length of the barrel and the impact of the shot, the effect of wind velocity on the weight of the slug, the parabola of a projectile at short range – none of which came close to the matter in hand: how to kill a man and kill him outright.

Jacinto Cruz seemed aware of it and, as if there were no one else around him, said to Ramón: 'Look, enough of all this crap; I'll tell you the best way to kill the Gypsy.'

His abrupt declaration silenced all the others. The Derringer faded into the background, and collective attention now centered on Jacinto and his proposal to Ramón. But, Jacinto said nothing about how, only asking Ramón to go with him. 'I have to show you how to kill him, because you won't understand if I just tell you.'

They left, followed by Pascual, Torcuato and Macedonio. Perplexed, the rest watched them depart, disguising their curiosity to know what Jacinto's proposition would be by returning to the limitations and advantages of a pistol like the .25 caliber double-barreled Derringer Davis, ten centimeters long.

2

The Gypsy awoke from his siesta gripped by apprehension that Gabriela might be murdered that very night. The premonition seemed ridiculous to him and he tried unsuccessfully to play it down. There were still unresolved matters in the air that might yet unleash unforeseen events. He was particularly disturbed by his ignorance of whether Pedro Salgado knew of his affair with Gabriela or not. Furthermore, he was intrigued by the identity of the murdered girl. Who was she? Why had she been knifed? For a moment he thought that she had been murdered by mistake and that the real victim was to have been Gabriela. Gabriela, Gabriela – even the thought of her name pained him, and why so intensely? Why was he unable to forget her as he had so many others? He had always enjoyed playing around with married women, bringing them to the razor's edge and then abandoning them at the very moment they were willing to run away with him. Why could he not do that with Gabriela?

He would have to go back for her as soon as possible; he could not stand another night thinking of her at a distance, dreaming of her, devoured by worms, desiring her furiously. Even so, he tried not to rush things. There was no point in going to Loma Grande that night; he would surely run into her husband and violence would be the outcome. Better to appear in the village on the following morning, after Pedro Salgado had left to pick cotton on the plantation, along with the other day laborers.

It occurred to him to thoroughly investigate the crime against Adela in Loma Grande. He ought not to enter the village uninformed. He supposed that Carmelo Lozano would know something and decided to visit the rural police headquarters at Ciudad Mante.

He left the Albatross in mid-afternoon, without seeing La Chata Fernández or her daughter, leaving the money for his bill in an envelope slipped under their door, with a laconic note:

Chata: You were right. Married women are better carried off. Best. José Echeverri-Berriozábal.

3

First, the group went to Jacinto's house, where the butcher collected some lengths of rope and a small sack.

'What's that?' asked Macedonio.

'A surprise,' answered Jacinto as he hung the sack

over his shoulder and handed a rope to each one of them.

They turned to the pastures below the southern slope of Bernal Hill. When they arrived, Jacinto asked for their help to find a reddish bull with a white forehead and only half a tail. Pascual found it grazing some distance away under a mesquite on the slope thickest with underbrush.

According to Jacinto, this was a very wild bull that had been wandering loose for a long time. 'He's really fierce,' he told them, 'so be careful.'

All five spread out to corral the bull, approaching as softly as possible to avoid startling it into flight. Hiding in the underbrush, Jacinto was able to get within a few paces. He crouched and threw his lasso, which hit the animal's back and slid off. The bull reacted by raising its horns and trotting off down the hill. Torcuato tried to head it off, but the bull lowered its head to charge and Torcuato jumped aside as it passed him.

'Cut him off over there,' yelled Jacinto to Ramón.

Ramón ran diagonally, trying to reach the animal, but the bull speeded up and disappeared into the undergrowth. Though they could hear it breaking branches and crushing bushes, it was hard to tell where it would appear. Jacinto, who knew the terrain well, guessed that it would break out on the upper slope of a dry gully and whistled to Pascual to go in that direction.

Pascual quickly crossed a clearing and hid behind a large nopal. He heard the animal thrashing in front of him and nervously prepared to lasso it. The bull broke out of the thicket heading towards the edge of the gully. Pascual waited and lassoed its legs as it passed. The animal bellowed at the feel of the rope and increased its speed. Pascual dug in his heels, trying to stop its advance, but the jerk only turned the bull in a circle to charge the man. Pascual rolled to avoid its horns, and the animal, in its momentum, slipped on the dry leaves and slid into the bottom of the gully.

Determined not to let it get away, Pascual wound the rope around his hands and allowed himself to be dragged along.

As it fell, the bull hit a rock sideways and turned over completely. Pascual tried to tie the lasso around a tree, but the furious animal bolted out of the dry gully, pulling him along.

From the slope, Torcuato, Jacinto and Ramón watched Pascual and the bull fall among the loose rock, and hurried down to help. Ramón arrived first and successfully lassoed the bull around the neck.

'Pull,' yelled Torcuato.

Ramón tightened the rope and the bull slowed its pace. When Torcuato reached the animal, he grabbed its tail. The bull turned, trying to use its horns, but Torcuato held tight to the tail and turned with the bull. Pascual stood up and tied his lasso to a tree trunk at the same time as Ramón. Finally tired out, the bull stopped fighting and stood still. Torcuato let go of the tail and got out of the way as quickly as possible. When Jacinto and Macedonio came up, all five turned the bull on its back to tie its feet together.

'The goddam animal must have been possessed by the devil,' remarked Pascual as he spat on the rope burns on the palms of his hands.

'Didn't I tell you he was wild?' laughed Jacinto.

A few meters away, the bull panted and snorted and shook its head, trying to get on its feet.

'I thought we could drive it to the corrals,' continued Jacinto, 'but we better give it to him right here.'

'And then what, we have to carry him away?' asked Macedonio.

'No way. I'll butcher him here and then come back for the meat with the mules,' answered Jacinto. He put the sack on his knees and added: 'Now, Ramón, I'll show you how to kill the Gypsy.'

He extracted an ice-pick and a knife-sharpener from the sack, filed the point of the ice-pick a few times and then tested it with his thumb. 'Ready,' he said.

He approached the fallen bull and felt along its ribs to a point close to the top of its foreleg and, marking the point with his index finger, said: 'This is where the heart is.'

The bull, sensing danger, bellowed fearfully and loud enough for the sound to reverberate off the sides of the gully. A long thick vein swelled in its neck and the hair on its back shivered.

Jacinto raised the ice-pick in his right hand and spread the folds of hide with his left.

'This is how it's done,' he said, and with barely visible speed sank the ice-pick into the animal's side. No sooner had he slowly withdrawn it than a spurt of blood sprang from the wound.

Dumbfounded by the execution, Ramón had no time to get out of the way and saw his shoes splashed with red. He felt dizzy imagining Adela bleeding like that.

'There's a hole right in his heart,' explained Jacinto. 'He'll be empty in no time.'

The bull watched them anxiously as the light went out of its eyes. Immobilized and dying, it seemed completely tame, quite unlike the furious beast that had fought them a few minutes before.

The fountain of blood rose and fell intermittently to the beat of its heart, until it became an unsteady flow. The bull snorted, expelling a clot through its nose, as the veins in its neck dilated until they disappeared. Finally, the animal stretched its head and hind legs for the last time until they dropped heavily.

Jacinto watched its last convulsions and, without looking at Ramón, asked: 'Did you get it?'

Ramón, imagining Adela dying in the same way, answered without thinking that he hadn't.

'Look,' continued Jacinto, 'if a bull this size dies that easily, imagine how fast you can deflate the Gypsy.'

Torcuato, who knew how difficult it was to slaughter goats and calves, marveled at the procedure. He would no longer have to search for the jugular to cut a goat's throat, nor find the cervical vertebrae to hack a calf's neck in two with a hatchet. Now all he needed was a clean, well-aimed stab with an ice-pick.

Macedonio was also full of enthusiasm: 'The Gypsy won't even know what he died of,' he said, convinced that the ice-pick was the perfect weapon for revenge: short and lethal.

Little by little, Ramón forgot Adela and concentrated on Jacinto's explanations.

'The trick,' added the butcher, 'is to stab hard, so if you hit bone, the point will slide off into the heart. That's why it has to be well sharpened.'

Jacinto stood next to Ramón and hid the ice-pick in his shirtsleeve.

'You'll have to hide it here,' he said extending his left arm, 'so the Gypsy won't see it, and when you're in position, you pull it out and drive it under his armpit.' He handed Ramón the ice-pick, saying, 'Let's see you do it.'

Ramón took the instrument by the handle and two or three times practiced the attack demonstrated by Jacinto.

'Now try it on the bull,' suggested Pascual.

Ramón turned to look at the enormous inert mass beside him.

'What for?'

'So that you get the hang of it,' added Jacinto.

Between them, they hoisted the carcass by its horns and hung it from the branch of an ebony.

'Stab at the ribs and cut through the bones,' ordered Jacinto.

Pascual pushed the carcass and set it swinging. Ramón struck, but the ice-pick barely entered.

'No, no, no,' scolded Jacinto. 'You've got to give it your whole arm. I'll show you.'

Jacinto took up a position beside the bull and Pascual swung it again. The butcher crouched and at the first swing stabbed violently, driving the ice-pick in up to the handle.

'You've got to put your balls into it. The way you're doing it, the Gypsy won't feel more than a tickle.'

Ramón made four more attempts until he was able to jab the ice-pick all the way into the carcass at the fifth. Then, to demonstrate his command of the technique, he did it three more times.

Jacinto patted the bull's rump and repeated to Ramón that he should stab the Gypsy in the armpit at the height of the left nipple.

'And once you've got it in, move it around inside so that it will tear up his guts.'

Macedonio was upset by Jacinto's calm, paternal assurance in his instructions to Ramón.

'Hey, Jacinto, how many customers have you knocked off?' he asked.

Without taking offense, Jacinto answered, 'Me? Not one,

but the guy who taught me how to slaughter cattle like that killed ten or more.'

No one believed him, but no more was said on the subject.

They cut open the bull and disemboweled it, Jacinto collecting the edible viscera – liver, lungs, stomach, kidneys – in plastic bags, and the testicles and tripe in a separate one. He showed them the heart pierced six times and handed it to Ramón.

'You've got good aim,' he said. 'Take it as a souvenir.'

They skinned the carcass and covered it with thorny huisache branches to protect it from coyotes. Jacinto salted the hide, rolled it up and tied it with a rope.

'I'll give you the hide if you lend me your grandfather's cart,' he suggested to Pascual. They agreed to return for the meat that night.

They were back in the village before dark. On the way, Ramón put his hand in his pocket several times to make sure that Adela's black-and-white, three-quarter-profile photograph was still there.

4

The Gypsy reached El Abra and stopped to buy oranges. He had not eaten anything but the morning's plate of beans. He sat on the hood of the pick-up and, peeling an orange with his teeth, sucked the juice from the segments and spat out the pulp. With a damp rag he wiped away the greenish-yellow blotches left by countless dragonflies on the windshield. He ate another orange and put the rest into an icebox.

Leaving El Abra, he took the federal highway to Ciudad

Mante, intending to find Carmelo Lozano. On the way, he remembered a Greek mariner he had known in his adolescence. The man had been the captain of a Liberian-registered freighter which stopped at Colón, Progreso, Coatzacoalcos, Veracruz, Tampico and Brownsville on its coastal run. He was known as 'Red Papadimitru', not for his red hair, which at forty was completely white, but for his boundless enthusiasm for communism.

He spoke correct Spanish, with a mixed foreign and tropical accent. He only lapsed into his native tongue when in a towering rage he would exclaim: '*Star gidia.*' He was famous in Tampico, among other things, for taking his exercise around the deck of his ship on a bicycle. The Gypsy had met him in a dockside joint where the betting was heavy on Spanish cards. Red Papadimitru rarely went there for the gambling, but often for a few drinks with his friends. He was a great conversationalist and enjoyed inventing outlandish theories on mundane matters. Many people gathered round him, including the Gypsy, just to listen to him.

On one of those many nights, Red Papadimitru made a remark that stuck in the Gypsy's mind. 'Some women,' he explained, 'are just bodies and others are people.' Someone pointed out that the distinction was infantile, that one way or another every woman was both a body and a person. Under the influence of a generous flow of whisky, Red clarified: 'Look, there are women you get into the sack, bang, and it's over, they slip by without a trace, forgotten the next morning. They're what I call bodies. On the other hand, there are women you can lay all your life and never finish making love to them. They're an endless handful of surprises. That's the kind I call a person. The first, you drop without wanting to know any more about them. But the others stay with you no matter how hard you try to get them out of your head.'

Red's explanation was received with whistles, applause and insults. He was accused of being a stud, a hayseed, a show-off, and a son of a bitch. The uproar had no effect on him; he just continued as always.

The Gypsy was so impressed by the man's ideas that he turned them over in his mind all night. He wondered if, from a woman's point of view, there were men who were just bodies and others who were people, and what happened if a man-body met with a woman-body, or a man-person with a woman-body and vice versa.

The following day he tried to show off the Greek's theories to his schoolmates, as if they were his own. It had not occurred to him that they might be turned against him until one of his schoolmates said: 'Then your mother is one of those body-women, because as far as I know your father screwed her for nothing and dropped her with you on the way.'

The Gypsy went livid with rage while his companions made fun of him. He tried to get even with his offender who, rather than face him, ran all around the schoolyard shouting, 'Come and see the son of a body-woman, come and see him . . .' Ashamed, the Gypsy left school and never went back.

He never returned to the joint either, and always hated the memory of Red Papadimitru. It gave him some satisfaction years later to learn that he had been found dead on the dock with the upper half of a tequila bottle jammed in his stomach, the work of a local prostitute: a body-woman.

He had not recalled the Greek's theories until that Tuesday afternoon, on his way to Ciudad Mante, when he realized that, no matter how often he made love to Gabriela,

138

there would never be an end to it. He could kiss her from head to foot without ever being satisfied, lick every inch of her skin and find a different flavor in each one. It was then, he thought, that he understood the Greek captain, that his remarks had not been mere male bravado, but the clumsy ruminations of a man who, obviously in love, was trying to distinguish his beloved from the rest of her kind.

5

When he reached Ciudad Mante, he drove across the city from one end to the other until he reached the exit for Ciudad Victoria. The rural police headquarters was located in the last house, almost on the highway.

He knocked on the door, which was opened by a sleepy cop in rumpled clothes reeking of beer.

'What's up, Gypsy? Come on in; the captain's in the bedroom.'

The Gypsy was in the habit of showing up once a month to pay his dues. He enjoyed a good reputation in the force as a reliable smuggler who paid up regularly and, except for his frequent troubles with married women, was never involved in brawls or disputes. He found Carmelo Lozano playing dominoes with three of his subordinates in a back room. Beside his chair lay several empty beer bottles of different brands, a bottle of cane liquor on the table next to a plate containing the remains of tacos. The room was lit by a bare bulb spotted with fly-shit. Bare to the waist, with a wet red rag over his shoulders, Lozano told the Gypsy to take a chair next to his.

'Give me a minute,' he said. 'Just let me block this guy's boxcar and I'll be with you.'

While the game went on, the Gypsy noticed two dead deer hanging from a beam in the patio.

'We confiscated them from some poachers,' explained Lozano. 'Tomorrow we're going to barbecue them. Wanna join us?'

'Na, I've got things to do,' answered the Gypsy, his eyes on the captain's dominoes.

Lozano turned one face up and spun it on the table. 'With this one I'm out,' he said.

And so it was. Another player put down a double four and the captain played his last, a four-two.

Lozano stood up and stretched till his hands touched the ceiling. 'Shuffle the pieces,' he ordered, 'while I see what my friend here wants.' He took a pull at the bottle and offered it to the Gypsy. 'What brings you here?' he asked.

'Life, Captain.'

Lozano grinned.

'And what else?'

'I've got business in Loma Grande and I heard there was trouble there . . . What do you know?'

'A girl was killed.'

'Yeah, I know,' interjected the Gypsy.

Lozano went right on: 'And the whole village is in an uproar.'

'How so?'

'Enough to do you in, if you show up.'

'Why me? I've got nothing to do with anything.'

Carmelo stretched again and dropped heavily into the chair. 'Vibes, my friend, vibes.'

He began another game.

'And what business do you have pending?' inquired Lozano.

'I've got to collect some debts.'

'Collect them another time.'

'I'm supposed to be paid tomorrow.'

Lozano picked up seven dominoes, straightened them and put them in numerical order. 'Will you look at this lousy hand,' he said, showing it to the Gypsy. Raising his head, he looked at his opponent: 'Who opens, you or me?'

The other man laid down a double three.

'I think you've got a thing going with some dame over there and you've got the hots.'

'There's truth in that, but I'm really going to collect the money.'

'If you want my advice, friend, don't go into the village. Honestly, they're mad as hell.'

'I just want to go and get paid. I'll be there and back on the same day.'

Lozano made a gesture of disapproval and slammed a domino on the table. 'Pass,' he said.

The hand went around and the captain passed again.

'Christ, pay attention to what I'm doing,' he reproached his partner.

'Next time around,' answered his subordinate nervously.

Lozano wiped the sweat off his face with the rag on his shoulders and took another pull at the bottle.

'OK, Gypsy, do what you want ... just don't come around crying to me afterwards.'

The game ended with Lozano and his partner losing by twenty-five points.

'Shit,' grunted Carmelo as he began to mix the dominoes again.

The Gypsy rubbed his hands tensely on his trousers.

'How about lending me a pistol, Captain? Just in case the worst comes to the worst and some nut in the village goes haywire,' he said, thinking of Pedro Salgado.

'No way,' exclaimed Lozano immediately. 'Who do you think I am? Furthermore, what do you need it for? Don't they say that you have the hide of a buffalo?'

'Yeah, but even cats run out of their nine lives.'

The captain turned to the Gypsy with a steady look.

'What are you afraid of, my friend? Didn't you say you have nothing to do with the matter?'

'And didn't you say that things at Loma Grande are serious?' answered the Gypsy calmly. 'I want the pistol just in case.'

Lozano seemed satisfied with the answer and changed his tone. 'I won't lend you one,' he said, and before the Gypsy could object, added, 'I'll sell it to you.'

'How much?' asked the Gypsy without hiding his satisfaction.

Lozano gave his three subordinates a look of complicity, and answered: 'Two thousand five hundred.'

'Shit, Captain, I could buy a shotgun for that.'

'That's the price, take it or leave it.'

The Gypsy put his hand in his pocket and felt the two thousand he had earned selling those tape recorders.

'I'll give you one-five.'

Lozano picked up his seven dominoes and, without taking his eyes off them, responded: 'I'll meet you halfway, two thousand two hundred.'

'One-seven.'

'One-nine and that's as far as I'll go.'

'Done.' The Gypsy took out his wad and counted out the bills on the table.

'There it is.'

The captain picked them up calmly and without counting stuck them in his shirt pocket.

They began another game and finished it, followed by another and another, without Lozano making a move. Impatiently, the Gypsy objected, 'What about the pistol?'

Feigning surprise, the captain answered: 'What pistol?'

The Gypsy groaned with anger and disappointment.

'For Christ's sake, Captain . . . don't give me that . . .'

'So help me, friend, I don't know what you're talking about,' said Lozano, looking inquiringly at his men. 'Do you know what he's talking about?'

The three cops shook their heads, smiling discreetly.

'You see, we don't know anything about a pistol.'

The Gypsy knew that when Lozano played dumb, there was no way around him.

'You're really going to take me for it?'

Carmelo Lozano put a domino down in the middle of the table.

'Double five,' he said, wiping his face with the damp rag again, and patted the Gypsy on the knee.

'Don't get me wrong, friend. I'm not cheating you, I'm helping you.'

'Screwing me out of my money?'

'No,' emphasized the captain, 'because the money you gave me is an advance on your dues, so beat it before you distract me and make me lose.'

The Gypsy was about to object, but Lozano cut him short: 'That's it, out! Because if you don't get out of here right now I'll charge you and lock you up.'

The Gypsy no longer insisted, but left the police headquarters in a rage. The captain had skinned him for almost two thousand pesos with no effort at all.

He drove back across the city to the highway to

Tampico, and parked on a side road. He got into the back, spread out a pad and a couple of sheets, and lay down to sleep. His mind was made up: trouble or not in Loma Grande, with or without a pistol, he was going to get Gabriela the following day.

CHAPTER XV

One Night Before

1

'The Gypsy is in Los Aztecas.'

The news reached the village via Guzmaro Collazos, who had just arrived on the bus that stopped at Loma Grande on Tuesday afternoon, on its route around El Abra – El Triunfo – Plan de Ayala – Niños Héroes – Los Aztecas – Ejido Madero – Díaz Ordaz – Canoas – Graciano Sanchez – Ejido Pastores – Loma Grande – Santa Ana – El Dieciocho – Lopez Mateos – Ciudad Mante.

'How do you know?' asked Amador Cendejas.

'I saw his pick-up in front of the rooming house,' answered Guzmaro, trying to revive one of his turkeys that had nearly suffocated under two sacks of sugar.

Marcelino, still angry from his argument with Justino Téllez, snapped, 'And you spilled the beans, didn't you?'

'There you go again,' whispered Justino so only those around them could hear.

Guzmaro stopped blowing into the failing turkey's beak and answered belligerently: 'Don't give me that shit, Huitrón. I'm no fag to be going around with gossip.'

'Well, you're the only one who left town after we figured out it was the Gypsy who killed the girl.'

So it was. That morning Guzmaro had cycled over to Niños Héroes to buy his turkeys. Leaving his bike with a cousin, he had come back by bus so as not to have to carry the birds.

'Well, I tell you, I never saw the Gypsy. All I saw, passing by, was his pick-up.'

'We'll see about that . . .' mumbled Marcelino.

Guzmaro made no further response to the provocation. The turkey had died in his hands and he didn't know what to do with it.

Knowledge that the Gypsy was close to Loma Grande excited a general impatience to kill him. Sotelo Villa proposed they go to Los Aztecas and lynch him. But Justino Téllez put a stop to it.

'That's not our business,' he said. 'It's up to Ramón.'

When Ramón returned from slaughtering the bull, he was eagerly awaited by the rest of the village men, who wanted to know how he would react to the Gypsy's presence only a few kilometers away. They pressured him in various ways: some making him repeat his vow to take revenge; others, the more aggressive, like Marcelino Huitrón and Sotelo Villa, urging him to go to Los Aztecas that very night, to get even. Confused, Ramón was at a loss to answer them, but Jacinto Cruz came to his aid.

'A good hunter lets his prey come to him, he doesn't go chasing it,' he said calmly.

The saying angered Marcelino Huitrón. 'What if he doesn't come?'

Justino Téllez interrupted without letting Jacinto respond, 'How many times do I have to tell you, Marcelino, that the Gypsy will be back?' he growled irritably.

'And how many times do I have to ask how the hell you know that?' Marcelino challenged him.

Justino rose from his chair, leaving his beer on the table and, facing Marcelino, said, 'Because a man with a clean conscience has nothing to fear,' and without further explanation turned and left.

The others were stunned; only Ranulfo Quirarte understood the delegate's remark perfectly. Obviously, Justino was as aware as he that the Gypsy was innocent, and others might know it as well as they. Ranulfo quailed at the feebleness of his lie. If Ramón did not kill the Gypsy, which was quite likely, the Gypsy would find out who had falsely accused him of the crime, and make him pay for it. There was no longer any way he could back out or undo the charade he had invented. Somehow, he had to ensure the Gypsy's sentence would be executed: it was his only hope.

He slipped nervously away from the crowd, to lie low at home and wait.

Night fell. Most of the crowd went home, leaving only a few in the shop. The atmosphere was heavy with the conviction that events would erupt at any moment.

Jacinto was convinced of it. He pulled Ramón aside. 'You've got to be prepared,' he told him, 'because the Gypsy won't be long in coming.'

Taking the ice-pick from his sack, he made a few passes with the sharpener. 'Ready,' he said, and handed it to Ramón, who took it with some reluctance.

'Don't think about it, just kill him without thinking about it.'

Ramón studied the point glinting in his hand. The time had passed for trial thrusts into the carcass of a dead animal or further blather. The wait for the moment of truth had begun.

CHAPTER XVI

The Last Chapter

1

He woke a little before dawn to the racket caused by a flock of blackbirds in the huisache over his pick-up. He had slept peacefully in spite of his anger at being swindled out of his money by Carmelo Lozano and the anticipation of soon having Gabriela Bautista in his arms again. Not even the overpowering heat shut into the airless cab of his pick-up had spoiled his rest.

The Gypsy opened the hatch, startling the entire flock into clattering departure. He stuck his head out to breathe the cool morning air and found it rank with the smell of burnt sugar cane. Sitting on the ice-chest, he put on his sneakers and got out of the cab. He could see the hump of Bernal Hill outlined against the morning shadows on the horizon. He would be crossing it before long.

He lit the portable primus stove to heat water for coffee. There was no hurry. He had to give Gabriela's husband time to leave for the cotton fields; by eight o'clock, his rival would be well away from Loma Grande. He made coffee with five teaspoons of sugar and one of powdered milk, the way his mother had done when he was a kid. She was convinced the sugar gave him energy and helped him grow faster.

Finishing the coffee, he sucked the juice out of two oranges, rinsed the coffee cup and poured the gas out of the stove into a glass jar. A coyote trotted past him, the two eyeing each other without fear or alarm as the animal went on its way.

On the radio, Tampico was broadcasting 'Good Morning Rancheros'. Two sleepy announcers were faking sparkling dialogue on the subject of letters received from 'faithful listeners'. After reading each one and praising the unqualified benefits of Bayer agricultural products, they announced the correct time.

When the Gypsy heard that Bayticol was the best remedy for ticks and that it was 7.15 a.m., he decided to depart. He put the stove into its case, rolled up the pad, folded the sheets and took an orange out of the ice-chest to suck on the way. Switching on the motor, he let it warm up, and then turned the wheel to back out onto the highway towards Tampico. He would reach his destination in forty minutes.

2

The first to witness his approach was Pascual Ortega, who recognized his pick-up in the distance, descending the slope from the dirt road to Number Eighteen. He studied the black dot on the road and, when he was sure who it was, left the pair of horses with which he was plowing his field, and lit out for the village.

Torcuato Garduño was loading sacks of corn onto a mule in his yard when he heard shouting. He climbed to the roof of his house to see Pascual desperately jumping furrows and yelling at the top of his voice, 'Here he comes, here he comes . . .'

Torcuato raised his eyes and spotted the pick-up heading toward the village. 'Holy shit,' he exclaimed.

He dropped from the corrugated roof, tied the mule to a post, and hurried to Jacinto Cruz' corral.

He found him, along with Macedonio, cutting out the steer they had slaughtered the day before.

'He's here,' he shouted.

'Who?'

Exasperated, Torcuato answered, 'The Gypsy ... who the hell do you think!'

Jacinto stood up and wiped the blood off his hands with a piece of newspaper. 'Is he here already?' he asked naturally.

'No, but he won't be long,' responded Torcuato impatiently.

Jacinto thought a moment.

'Go tell Ramón, tell him to get ready; that the Gypsy's here and that I'll take him to the store.'

Torcuato got his instructions, jumped the corral fence, and ran with the news.

'And you,' said Jacinto to Macedonio, 'gather up as many as you can and hang out near the store in case things get ugly.'

Macedonio headed for the fields to gather the others. Jacinto wrapped the meat and put it into a burlap bag. He stuck his cutting-out knife into its sheath, and slipped it inside his shirt. He figured the best way to intercept the Gypsy was to wait for him outside Rutilio Buenaventura's house, where the Gypsy would surely go first of all, and then invite him to Ramón's store for a beer.

He went through the gate to the lot and saw Pascual running into the village, yelling, 'Here he comes, here he comes ...'

3

Justino Téllez put the glass of milk back on the table and pushed himself back in his chair. He had heard Pascual's warning cries and the murmuring that followed them. Now he could hear the rumble of the Gypsy's approaching pick-up.

He closed his eyes. He had heard that peculiar sound that precedes a violent death many times before. It was the same sound he had heard the morning the three Jiménez brothers murdered Nazario Duarte; the same sound he had heard the night Rogaciano Duarte torched Hipólito Jiménez' hut in revenge, reducing it to ashes along with its owner, his wife and two daughters; the same sound the afternoon eight undercover cops had ambushed Adalberto Garibay and riddled him with lead, mistaking him for a drug-dealer. The same sound: running steps in the dust, voices, men back and forth, and then a ragged silence. In short, a sound you can only hear in your head.

He picked up the glass and gently swirled its contents. He contemplated the milk sticking to the walls of the glass and then sliding viscously down. He could, at that very moment, go out onto the highway and warn the Gypsy of the imminent attack. He could go to Ramón's store and make it clear to Ramón that the Gypsy had nothing whatever to do with the crime against his girlfriend, if Adela was indeed his steady girl, and that the same man who had had sex with her minutes before her death was the one who had stuck the knife in her, and that it wasn't worth avenging her by spilling innocent blood. He could, in front of all of them, reveal the secret game of the real murderer, who quite probably was instigating the circumstances their would bring about the mortal encounter between

Ramón and the Gypsy. He could, once and for all, silence the sounds of impending violent death that were boring into his ears. But he did none of those. He just sat and watched the milk slide down the sides of the glass.

4

She undressed and poured several glasses of water over her hair, letting the water run over her torso to refresh it. She would have to overcome yet another morning of heat and dust.

She switched on the portable radio and turned up the volume. Sitting on the bed to brush her hair, she hummed along with the cumbia on the radio, until she finished brushing. Looking into the mirror, she could see tiny, almost imperceptible wrinkles around her eyes, which made her frown with disappointment. Long ago, her grandmother had told her that women who began to show wrinkles were like fruit that was beginning to rot. That was a lie: she had begun to rot long before.

She left the mirror and went to the kitchen cupboard; she was hungry. As she passed the window, she saw Pascual Ortega through the gauze curtains, running in the distance past the school windows. He was yelling something, but she could not make out what it was, over the noise of the radio. She turned it down, but could no longer hear him, and stood thoughtfully for a moment. Suddenly the sound of an automobile motor reached her. She pricked up her ears: it was unmistakable. She pulled back the curtain, not caring that she might be seen naked from the street, and stuck her head out, trying to hear where the sound was coming from. When she turned to the right, her heart pounded: his black pick-up was turning the corner.

Delighted, Gabriela jumped to the bed and pulled out her box of clothes. She began to dress hurriedly and suddenly stopped.

'They're going to kill him,' she exclaimed out loud.

She wrapped a sheet around herself and ran to the door. She had to head him off, warn him that they were going to kill him, tell him they ought to run away together. She heard him lean on the horn three times: the signal that he would meet her at the usual place in half an hour. Anguished, she pulled the bolt and yanked open the door.

Realizing the Gypsy was accelerating, in despair she ran out half-naked to try to catch him, and shouted, 'Gypsy!' but nothing more, because Ranulfo Quirarte, leaning against a lamppost, asked her what she wanted.

5

He stopped in front of Rutilio Buenaventura's house, turned off the motor, and sat with his hands on the wheel. Everything seemed quiet to him, but he had better be cautious. Carmelo Lozano was not the kind to issue idle warnings. He cranked down the windows so that air could circulate and cool the cab, and got out. He walked to the entrance to Rutilio's lot, and gave him his usual warning whistle. There was no answer from the old man.

'He's asleep.'

The Gypsy spun around towards the voice behind him and met Jacinto Cruz' friendly smile.

'I came looking for him too,' added Jacinto, 'but he

doesn't answer ... he hasn't even put the chickens out yet.'

That was the first thing Rutilio did when he woke up – let the chickens loose – and they could still be heard squawking inside the house.

Jacinto Cruz took off his hat to wipe away the sweat dripping onto his forehead.

'The sun's already scorching,' he said. 'Why don't we go have a beer till the old man gets up? On me.'

The Gypsy turned down the offer: 'I'd sooner wait here.'

But Jacinto persisted, patting him on the back: 'Why sweat it? Sometimes Rutilio doesn't get up till nine or ten. Ah, c'mon, we won't be long.'

The Gypsy had no reason to be suspicious of Jacinto. On earlier visits to Loma Grande, they had even got drunk together.

'Just let me take a look inside to see if he's awake yet,' he said and, pushing the gate open, stepped into the lot.

Nervously, Jacinto watched him go to the house. Rutilio could warn him and spoil the whole plan.

The Gypsy peered through the window and came back.

'He's asleep in the rocker.'

'So whadaya say?'

'All right, let's go.'

6

Four times he picked up the ice-pick and four times put it down. It was an entirely different ice-pick from the one he had grasped the previous afternoon. It was shaped differently, had another texture, other proportions. This one was ungraspable, didn't fit in the hand.

In desperation Torcuato watched Ramón's futile efforts to hide the ice-pick inside the left cuff of his shirt.

'Hurry up,' he barked.

Ramón picked it up again, trying to steady his fingers, but couldn't. He put it down on the counter again.

'You're backing out,' roared Torcuato.

He wasn't; he just couldn't find a way to hide the weapon in the folds of his sleeve. Nor could he find a way to stop the pounding pulse in his temples, or loosen up the cramped muscles in his forearm. Torcuato had brought the news too soon. He couldn't prepare himself to kill, or be killed, so suddenly. No, not like that.

Torcuato tried to settle the ice-pick inside Ramón's shirt, but so roughly that it fell to the floor. Suddenly Macedonio appeared in the doorway and whispered, 'Here they come.'

Ramón scooped up the ice-pick in his right hand and grasped it with all his might. He would not let go of it again.

Peeping through a hole in the wall, Torcuato saw Jacinto and the Gypsy approaching.

'Have you let the air out of his tires?' he asked.

Macedonio nodded, and Torcuato turned back to watch.

'They're passing Marcelino's house,' he said. Ramón clamped his jaws and took a deep breath.

'Don't let him get away,' said Torcuato as he and Macedonio slipped out to hide.

Ramón stepped behind the counter, covered the ice-pick with a cloth and held it as low as possible.

7

The clues that alerted the Gypsy's intuition to a surprise attack were minimal, barely perceptible: curious glances from women peeping out of windows as he passed, men surreptitiously slipping from one corner to another, and a ragged silence that was unusual for the village at that hour of the morning.

Without becoming too alarmed, the Gypsy prepared to face any assault, tensing his muscles and carefully studying every corner.

When they reached the store, he immediately stood with his back to the counter. He wanted the entrance before him so that he could spot any strange movement. He cared nothing for Ramón behind him, the storekeeper was no danger to him at all.

Jacinto said a clipped 'Good day', which Ramón, breathless, was unable to answer. He was trying to control the trembling that shook him from head to toe.

Jacinto took two beers from the cooler and opened them. 'We're going to have a couple of beers,' he said to Ramón with a conspiratorial smile, and turned to hand the Gypsy one of them. The Gypsy took it with his left, keeping his right free for whatever was going to happen.

Jacinto took a pull at his bottle and leaned against the wall next to the doorway. The Gypsy kept an attentive eye on him.

They began to chat. Ramón, still behind the counter, was unable to control his nerves. Outlined against the light from the door, the Gypsy looked taller and stronger than he remembered. He thought he could never kill him.

Jacinto, anxious about the boy's nervousness, finished his beer and asked for another. Ramón guessed that was the signal to act. He came around the counter towards the cooler to pass in front of the Gypsy, and shivered. The man straightened up to let him pass.

Ramón stopped next to the cooler, just to the left of the Gypsy. The ice-pick vibrated between his fingers. He raised his eyes and glimpsed the spot where he would thrust it. Slowly, he let the cloth fall away, leaving the ice-pick visible.

His attention on the doorway, the Gypsy did not realize that Ramón was armed. He raised the bottle in his left hand to take a drink. Ramón saw the sweat stain under his armpit and aimed for it, sinking the ice-pick into it up to the handle and pulling it out again in one motion.

At the blow, the Gypsy staggered two steps and grasped a shelf to steady himself. He felt a sharp hot pain in his side and lifted his hand to the hole in his armpit. It came away wet and he raised it, surprised to see it dripping red, as if doubting that the blood was flowing from himself. He felt the would again, looking at Ramón.

'You son of a whore,' he murmured.

Brandishing the beer bottle, he smashed it furiously against the counter. Frightened, Ramón backed off, grasping the ice-pick, ready to attack. The Gypsy shook his head, sucked a lungful of air and, as his chest swelled, the bloodstain spread in a circle on his shirt. Giddy with death, he walked the three meters to the doorway and, swaying, held on to the frame. He looked out at a couple of women staring at him in consternation.

'No more,' he gasped, and gasped again for air. Then he clenched his fists, his face distorted with pain, and collapsed slowly forward as if he were bending over to pick up a coin from the floor, until he fell heavily onto the dry dust of the street.

Ramón slid along the counter and watched the Gypsy's last gasp from inside the store.

8

The body lay face down, sweaty cheek squashed into the dust, eyes open, looking sideways. Jacinto approached it and put the palm of his hand under the nose to see if there was still any breath.

'Is he still alive?' asked Torcuato, arriving along with Macedonio and Pascual to surround the corpse.

'No,' answered Jacinto laconically. He stood up and entered the store, to find Ramón pale and trembling.

'You've got to get away from here,' he ordered.

Ramón looked at him apprehensively.

'Where to?'

'Anywhere, but beat it now.'

'Why?'

Jacinto did not answer. From his silence, Ramón understood that his departure was inevitable. He opened a box under the counter and, taking all the money there was in it, went out into the street.

He studied his enemy's body for a moment and then began to run.

Having watched the murder through her crack in the wall, the widow Castaños emerged nervously from the house to see her son disappear into the distance.

9

He ran and ran along path after path, finally stopping when his legs gave out, to sit on a rock and rest. He was far from Loma Grande, far beyond the Pastores Ejido. He examined the bloody ice-pick still in his hand, and cleaned it with saliva until no sign of blood remained. Then he shoved it into his belt.

The morning seemed to him empty of all its usual features. The heat was no longer the same as every day, nor the breeze, nor the chirping of the cicadas. Something had changed everything and made it different.

He was thirsty and hungry. It seemed a mistake not to have fled along the path bordering the Guayalejo river. There at least he would have had access to water and could have stolen crayfish from the traps. Now the river was several kilometers away.

He walked through a rock-strewn field, looking for something to eat. Finally, in a stand of sorghum he stripped a handful of seeds from a plant, first testing them with the tip of his tongue for insecticide. It was the season for private growers to hire crop-dusters. The seeds weren't bitter, indicating that they were free of insecticide, and he devoured them by the handful.

Leaving the sorghum, he checked the position of the sun and headed north, thinking it best to go to his brother in Kansas.

He walked along a dirt road for several minutes and suddenly stopped, searching vainly in his pockets for Adela's photograph. It was not there. He wanted to go back to Loma Grande and risk everything for her once more. Then it seemed crazy. After all, who was Adela? He headed north again, but after a few paces stopped again:

Adela was everything and he could not forget her, simply couldn't. He turned around to see Bernal Hill in the distance, and began to walk south, moving faster and faster. Soon he would have Adela again, be it only in the shape of a wrinkled, three-quarter-profile, black-and-white photograph.